BETWEEN MALES

Between Males

Fiona Walker

CORONET BOOKS

Hodder & Stoughton

Copyright © 2000 Fiona Walker

First published in 2000 by Hodder & Stoughton
First published in paperback in 2001
A Coronet paperback
A division of Hodder Headline

10 9 8 7 6 5 4 3 2 1

A CIP catalogue record for this title is available
from the British Library

ISBN 0 340 68229 9

Typeset by Palimpsest Book Production Limited,
Polmont, Stirlingshire

Printed and bound in Great Britain by
Mackays of Chatham plc, Chatham, Kent

Hodder & Stoughton
A division of Hodder Headline
338 Euston Road
London NW1 3BH

For the two women to whom I owe Odette and gratitude – the sultry-voiced Kensington High Flyer and the simply amazing Queen's Park Arranger.

Appetiser

Appetiser

'I've made you and Mr H some cinnamon muffins, Mrs H.'

'Ah, that's really sweet of you, Max. Would you bring them up?'

'Sure thing, Mrs H. Get off the couch, Freeway.'

On screen, Stephanie Powers replaced the receiver and snuggled up to Robert Wagner, her satin pyjama top rustling. *'I hope you're hungry, Jonathan darling.'*

He looked up from his paper. *'After the week we've had, darling, I guess we've both worked up an appetite.'*

They both dissolved into laughter and the credits rolled.

Odette hit the rewind button on the run as she crossed from kitchen to bathroom, clutching an Evian bottle. She'd worked up quite an appetite, too, but she had no intention of ruining it by eating just yet.

She had just spent two wonderful days punishing herself for her excesses. She had almost forgotten the pleasure of the castigation diet, which worked best after a truly shameful blow-out, or in this case a suck-in. The only things to enter her mouth since Barfly's enthusiastic tongue had been a toothbrush and the circular rim of an Evian bottle. She felt good as a result – leaner than ever, suitably purged and ready for the party of the year.

Working in advertising, Odette knew that all PR parties were the party of the year. In fact there were more than 365 parties of the year each year, sometimes several each night. Tonight's launch of celebrity chef Wayne Street's cookbook was mercifully unrivalled by other high-profile celebrations, premières and openings, but it hardly stood out. It was mid-week and mid-summer, not a great time to show off next week's *Times* Bestseller List Number One. But the publishers were confident that those big buyers and media pundits not on holiday would come, lured by the promise of delectable Street fare. And Odette, who'd had a peek at the guest list, was excited enough to have called Selena at Harvey Nicks. Her trusty personal shopper had picked out a gem of understated and cool linen chic. When the courier had dropped the dress off, Odette had e-mailed Selena with the one line: *Just up my Street.*

She loved e-mail. It fitted perfectly into her hectic schedule and allowed her to stay in touch with those friends she simply had no time to contact during working evenings and weekends. But she supposed it was a sign of post-millennium syndrome that she was only in regular communication with friends who were on-line. Other classic symptoms were mindlessly dialling 9 for an outside line on your home phone and trying to enter your password into the microwave. Odette habitually did both, although she was determined that this was going to change. As soon as she was her own boss, she vowed that she would see more of her friends, her flat and her family. Well, maybe not her family.

Her friends often joked that the only times Odette ever sat down were when she was on the loo or in the car. Tonight was no exception. She raced around her flat spraying on scent and clipping on earrings, ignoring the phone, which she'd turned on to auto-answer while her ten-minute *Hart to Hart* fix was playing in the background.

'Darling, it's Elsa. I'm *dying* to know what happened after you got back to London on Sunday. Jez says you and that big hunk kissed all the way home in the back of his car. And you keep saying you have no time for men these days, you liar! Are you bringing him to Juno's comedy gig tomorrow night? If so I'll need to try and get another ticket, and I think it's sold out. Call me tonight if you can.'

Odette looked at her watch guiltily. Calling Elsa straight back would make her late, and she wasn't quite ready to joke about her embarrassing lapse of judgement the previous weekend. She'd been more than a little drunk, in celebratory mood, and the

Glenns' sunny garden had seemed the ideal setting for a bit of reckless flirtation. But she should never have let brawny Barfly kiss her, let alone have travelled back to London with him. She'd dumped him as soon as Jez had dropped them off at a tube station. Thankfully, Barfly had been so keen to make last orders at his local pub, she doubted he was any more love-struck than she was. She had no intention of seeing him again in her entire life.

It was a rare slip, and Odette wanted to forget it as quickly as possible. Just as her meticulously practised Standard English accent occasionally lapsed into more familiar Stepney tones during moments of crisis, so Odette's taste in men veered between the dapper, urbane public school businessman she longed to capture and the back street bad-boys she seemed to attract. Barfly was eighteen stones of East End prejudice, the sort of man Odette had grown up with and with whom her mother would like her to settle down, just as her elder sister had. Kissing him had been a fairly unpleasant experience – something akin to having one's mouth full of lukewarm Peshwari Naan bread in an Indian restaurant after too many lagers. Thus the castigation diet had been called into play. Barfly probably thought castigation was something vets did to stop dogs breeding.

The party for *Street's Ahead* was being held at the private club, Office Block, where Wayne Street was one of three hundred handpicked members. He had also been its executive chef before he developed his current aversion to any kitchen that wasn't located in a television studio.

Wayne Street was big news right now. The three Michelin-starred media darling, commonly known as Meal Ticket, was everywhere. He currently appeared on every panel quiz and food programme that the networks could churn out, he'd toured the country with a huge stadium-filling road show, *Street Live*, and had his own prime-time cookery series, *Eat Street*, which had given rise to his first million-selling book. He was such a hit he made Delia look like Fanny Craddock. He also had a national newspaper column, a well-documented relationship with a page-three girl, and had even starred as himself in a recent Brit-pack film about a restaurant. On top of that, he fronted the hugely successful advertising campaign for British Beef, which Odette had produced and which had miraculously increased sales against all odds, earning her a vast bonus and Wayne a further nickname, Beefcake. It was also sometimes rumoured that he still worked as a chef in three restaurants, although few people had ever spotted him there.

In return for earning him close to half a million, Odette had sought Wayne's advice in recent months. She wanted to start a restaurant; Wayne was just the man to ask. He had made it clear from the start that he was far too busy to be of any hands-on help, but his expertise and business know-how were invaluable. Tonight he had promised to introduce her to a number of helpful contacts. She was officially entertaining the man who had commissioned the beef ad, but was certain she could name-check the right people in less time than it took to cook a minute steak. When it came to mingling, Odette worked faster than vodka through Red Bull.

She couldn't wait to have a look inside Office Block. It had recently taken over from the legendary Nero in terms of chichi chic, and the wait to be placed on its membership list was said to be longer than the careers of most of the stars on it. She longed to receive the hallowed invitation to take up membership at a grand a year, but she was way too unimportant. It didn't matter that she was one of the country's top-ranking commercials producers with inches of media-page copy dedicated to her in the broadsheets, a six-figure salary, great contacts and a Midas touch for selling coal to Geordies, bacon to Israelis and washing powder to housewives. She was still nobody in Office Block terms. Again, she was certain this would change when she owned a restaurant of equally glamorous proportions on the other side of London.

Leaving her beloved Beamer in an NCP car park, she checked her reflection briefly in the darkened windows – immaculate – before heading for Office Block with her hallowed invitation tucked into her neat little bag along with her mobile, electric organiser, lipstick and keys. The place was already buzzing, although it looked more like a model casting for a pop promo than a publishing party. Odette's smile clicked easily into place as she made her way towards the party's epicentre to say hello to Wayne. Then the smile wavered as she heard a familiar voice.

'You trollop!' came a delighted call.

Odette felt herself stiffening uncharitably as she looked around for the telltale mane of white-blonde hair. Lydia Morley, with her beauty and flirtatious charm, was a blatant freeloader. It was typical of her to be here. Odette wasn't surprised, but she resented the fact, and not just because she had only earned her own invitation after so much hard work and persistence. Odette hated to mix business with pleasure; she liked to keep the two as separate as starter and dessert, skipping the main course of love and marriage until she had more appetite for it. Juno's friend Lydia had been at the scene of Odette's recent badly judged coupling. Being as discreet as a tabloid headline, she was bound to mention Barfly and embarrass Odette in front of a host of potential contacts.

'Odie, darling!' Lydia floated over, towing a familiar-looking tall blond man behind her. 'I might have guessed you'd be here networking like a mainframe. Have you met my new boyfriend, Finlay?'

Eyeing the beautiful, gap-toothed blond man, Odette vaguely remembered meeting him through Juno, who was known to her friends as the Social Engineer. Finlay seemed sweet enough, if a little spacey, but Odette guessed he wouldn't be around long. Lydia changed lovers more often than she changed her mind over what was the new black, which was almost as often as she changed sheets, jobs, knickers or trains.

'Good to meet you, Finlay babes.' Odette held out her hand to shake, thus cutting him off as he swooped to kiss her cheek. She liked to take control when first introduced to men, who generally greeted her remarkable breasts before looking at her unremarkable face. But Finlay was thankfully far too besotted with Lydia's tiny, taut cleavage to leer at Odette's mammoth assets.

'Isn't this fun?' Lydia was giggling. 'Finlay came down to

Devon today to rescue me from a sex workshop, didn't you, darling?'

Odette's eyebrows shot up. Knowing Lydia's reputation, she was hardly in need of lessons.

'I'm going to become a Psycho-sexual Counsellor,' Lydia explained. 'I was attending a Dealing with Impotency course. Terribly dull. You both have to sleep in your pants for months, apparently.'

'And Finlay rescued you?' Odette, who slept in a singlet and pants, felt very naff.

'He says I can practise on him,' Lydia giggled. 'But he brought me to this party instead. We're having petit-four play.'

Finlay coughed hard, looking tetchy and unsettled, and Odette suddenly noticed his crusty nose. That was either a cold or one hell of a coke habit. She guessed the latter. No wonder he wanted to party at Office Block; it was nicknamed Charlie Echo because the sound of sniffing reverberated around the long corridors in the basement.

'Tell me, darling,' Lydia brushed imaginary crumbs off Odette's dress, 'what does one wear to hand in one's resignation? I know you're the right person to ask. Something understated and virginal like this little dress of yours – is it Donna Karan by the way? Or something a little sexier that says fuck you?'

Odette didn't like the way this conversation was going. She doubted Lydia knew about her own recent decision – they weren't very close friends, after all. In fact Lydia still mistakenly believed that Odette was a voracious sexual predator, a myth Juno, Elsa and Jez loved to tease her about. Nothing could be further from the truth.

'Aren't you working with Juno at Immedia?' Odette was trying to look discreetly around the room to check out who she could hastily introduce them to before moving on. She had a lot of work to do. Thankfully, the beef ad man hadn't arrived yet.

'Yes – in fact they've just offered me Joo's job,' Lydia said without a trace of guilt. 'They say she's rather lost her edge. But, you know, I don't think I'm cut out for the nine-to-five. You're lucky that you love it so much, Odie darling.'

'I'd hardly call my job nine-to-five.' She bristled, grabbing a glass of fizzy water from a roving drinks waiter. 'I have a broad brief.'

'You don't need broad briefs, sugar.' Finlay openly admired her pert backside. As he had ignored her boobs, this was a move calculated to make Odette adore him. She hated the fact that her bottom – which she'd worked very hard to achieve – was continually overlooked for her chest, which had arrived by an accident of birth. She smiled at him warmly and decided Lydia had chosen wisely. Shame about the habit, but it went with the territory these days. If a London man got out his credit card on the first date, he was generally planning to cut some coke. That was one of the many reasons Odette had given up dating long ago.

'What do you do?' he asked.

'I produce commercials,' she said proudly. It was a boast she'd have to forgo soon, although her new boast would be far better: 'I'm opening a restaurant.'

When Finlay gave her a curious look, Odette checked herself in horror. She hadn't said it aloud, had she? Christ, she had! She thought she'd kicked the habit.

'Oh, how thrilling!' Lydia gasped. 'You're junking your job too! Is that why you're here? Don't tell me you're planning to ask Wayne Street to be your chef?'

Odette peered around to check that they couldn't be over-heard by any of her colleagues. It was true she had handed in her resignation just a week ago, but news of her desertion was still being kept secret because she was such a feather in the agency's cap. If it leaked out before a replacement was found, half the staff might walk. She cursed herself for being a show-off.

'Breaking out of the rat race is very *now*, very New Millennium,' Lydia carried on blithely. 'Everyone in the know is turning their backs on the security of a fat salary and going it alone. It's fashionable. You're so clever, Odette. Fin's just junked in his job for me, haven't you, Fin?' She said it as though he'd bought her a diamond ring. Odette guessed she must be hopelessly out-of-touch to want a strong, solvent man. Nowadays it seemed the ultimate date was a man who abused strong solvents.

'Sure have, sugar.' He was looking at Lydia with total devotion. Most men would throw themselves off cliffs for the ravishing, platinum-blonde temptress. Odette preferred the more subtle method of making them throw themselves off boardroom balconies after she'd taken away their blue-chip clients.

'Well, I'm working tonight,' she put in smartly, realising she'd have to down play things dramatically. 'And I'd appreciate it if you didn't mention the restaurant thing to anyone. It's nothing. Just a pipe-dream, babes.'

'I see – you haven't got the money together yet.' Lydia nodded, pretending she understood, big blue eyes awash with seductive sympathy. Realising, at least, that Odette was calling for a change of subject, she added, 'Did you enjoy Joo's party, darling? I thought it was rather last year – all that sing-along eighties nostalgia. I left early. Did I spot you getting *very* chummy with that big—'

Suddenly Odette spotted Calum Forrester with relief. She could pass Lydia and Finlay on to him. She didn't know him too well, but Calum was a Glaswegian like Finlay, and famous enough to excite Lydia. And it would do Odette no harm to reintroduce herself, she realised happily.

The notorious millionaire maverick of the restaurant world was belligerently holding a can of McEwan Export that clearly stated 'I belong here and can do what I like'. He was talking to a small, cheerful brunette whose friendly expression belied a frantic need to escape. Her glass was empty and Calum's rudimentary social skills – looking over her shoulder and yawning in an arrogant display of mock-boredom – didn't seem to be endearing him to her. Odette had received much the same treatment whenever they'd met. Earlier this year she'd approached him about her restaurant idea but, after an initial burst of enthusiasm over the phone, he had failed to attend a single meeting and had never produced the promised investment.

'Calum!' She drew him over with easy skill. 'Odette Fielding.'

When he looked at her blankly, she added, 'We sat together at the Ad-Awes last month.' The advertising world's Oscars were nick-named the Ad-awes or Adores, and Odette had picked up a top award. But by then Calum – who'd been seeing one of the

10

models from the ad – had sloped off to the pub, leaving his date in tears. It was a gentle break-up by his standards.

He was now, predictably, looking at her boobs in faint recognition, pale grey eyes narrowed thoughtfully. He was one of the few people who made Odette feel uncomfortably hot and ruffled when he did so.

The Adores was only the latest of many encounters, but he never remembered her. Whether this was deliberate or not, she was uncertain. He had the intentional arrogance of a young rock-star matched with the absent-minded, careless indifference of an old professor. In fact, Calum Forrester embodied the ageing New Lad, a stereotype which confused Odette. His style was currently Über-vogue amongst men, much imitated by her advertising cronies. He was as happy at a cutting-edge modern art exhibition as a car show. He played pro-celebrity football with British film stars and lunched in the City with Michael Green and Richard Branson. He was forever being featured in *GQ*, *FHM* and *Loaded*, and yet he only read the *Financial Times* and the *Sunday Sport*. He dressed like a Manchester hooligan and shopped at Versace. Odette thought of him as an expensive lager commercial – all style, contradiction and money, oblique and complicated, yet essentially selling tasteless fizz to a bunch of eager punters whose only desire was drunkenness. Calum's super-cool restaurants and clubs sold the illusion of cloistered clique chic to the Beautiful Ones, and Odette was one of many eager punters who bought into it big time. She admired his genius, however rude his attitude.

'Yeah, sure – hello, Odette,' he said vaguely, slurping from his can then wiping froth from his lip with the back of his hand. Manners had never been his strong point, although he managed to introduce his companion. 'This is Jilly Reed.'

'Julie Wright,' the woman corrected kindly, giving Odette a grateful smile. Recognising an ally, Odette wanted to link Calum up with Lydia and Finlay so that they could both break free as quickly as possible.

'Julie, Calum, this is Lydia Morley and Finlay . . . I'm sorry, I didn't catch your second name?' She looked at the blond

11

Scot. He was, to her astonishment, giggling inanely. Bloody coke-heads, Odette thought darkly.

'Forrester,' he snorted. 'I'm Finlay Forrester. Calum and I are brothers. We live together – which reminds me, we're out of tea bags, bro.'

Odette felt an unattractive blush glow beneath her immaculately applied makeup. She might not like the way Calum had snubbed her in the past, but he was one of the most powerful figures at this party and she'd just committed an embarrassing blooper by introducing him to his own brother. She was a proud person, and self-deprecation didn't come easily to her. She knew she should laugh it off right now, just as she should laugh off the Barfly encounter, but instead she felt humiliated and stupid.

Lydia quickly went on a charm offensive. 'Calum, how gorgeous to meet you. I had no idea Fin's big brother was *the* Calum Forrester. Of course, now I can see the family resemblance.' This was a blatant lie as Calum was as short and charismatically ugly as Finlay was tall and beautiful, although they shared the same B & H packet blond hair and Meccano-sharp bone structure. But Finlay's hair was deliciously curly and his bones fleshed out with golden skin, whereas Calum's face was as lean as a skull and his hair was an unkempt tangle that receded at the temples. He generally wore a trademark leather pork-pie hat, but tonight it was far too hot. Drops of sweat were already lining up in the creases of his forehead like beads on an abacus.

He looked deeply uncomfortable, scuffing his feet and shooting his brother dirty looks. 'You kept quiet about this one, wee bree.'

'We only got together this afternoon,' Lydia laughed. 'We haven't even fucked yet, have we, my darling?'

At this, Finlay turned a surprising shade of pink.

Odette was mortified by her friend's behaviour. 'I – er – ugh,' she coughed, desperate to get away. 'Need to talk to . . .'

Julie caught her eye. 'Me too!'

'Talk to who?' Lydia looked at them both curiously, totally unaware she had said anything embarrassing.

'Wayne,' Odette managed to splutter.

'The very man,' Julie nodded in agreement. 'I'd love to meet him.' She gave Odette a conspiratorial wink.

Odette clicked into professional mode, intensely grateful for the opportunity to escape. 'Sure, I'll introduce you. Excuse us.' She left Lydia with the Forrester brothers, her friend still clearly astonished that her beautiful young Lancelot with his naughty nose habit and exquisite dress sense could be related to the gnome-like restaurateur with his famous friends and notorious lack of style.

'Thanks,' Julie muttered as they rushed away. 'That Calum's a jerk, isn't he? After all I've read about him in the papers, I thought he'd be a laugh, but he's just dead boring.'

'Terminal,' Odette agreed, glancing over her shoulder. There was something fascinating about Calum, though, even if she couldn't exactly figure it out. Perhaps that was the fascination. He was one of the few men she had ever met in whom she couldn't pinpoint a weak spot. Unlike Lydia, who could make men melt in to devoted submission with her beauty alone, Odette knew her skill was to sell them things. Calum had refused to buy her idea and it irritated her more than she wanted to admit.

'She's good, isn't she?' Finlay sat observing the party from a pony-skin chair in a dark corner as he and Lydia alternately kissed and people-watched. They were, he thought dreamily, made for one another, loving exhibitionism and voyeurism in equal measure.

Odette was showing the man from the Meat Council a wild time. He was hardly an easy guest – small, scurfy, with nervous darting eyes and a permanently wet upper lip – yet he had met the most important people at the party on an equal level, stayed awash with champagne, fattened himself on exquisite nibbles and laughed happily all evening, courtesy of Odette. Meanwhile, she had still discreetly managed to talk to the publishing house's head of marketing about getting book adverts on television – a rarity which she planned to turn around before she left the company. They had a meeting scheduled for the following week, along with another she had hastily set up with Wayne

Street while the meat man was in the lavatory, to talk about his facing up a credit-card commercial. That involved seriously big money, and she liked Wayne, although she instinctively felt the more temperamental, sexy chef Florian Etoile was a better option. Wayne was suffering just a little from over-exposure. He was, Odette privately suspected, about to become Wayne on the wane.

On top of all this, she had made some seriously good contacts for her restaurant, which she planned to chase up in her own time.

Finlay knew none of this, but he could see the way she operated and it was like watching a glamorous big cat circling a herd of impala, picking them off one by one with deadly, mesmerising skill.

Lydia, who was growing bored, was miffed by his obvious admiration. 'Yes, she's very professional – although Joo says she slept her way into her job. Total nympho apparently,' she yawned, longing to lure Finlay back to her flat. But he seemed keen to stick around at the party, just like his brother.

Calum was standing nearby, talking to a stunning reporter who was clearly smitten. Lydia had heard that he had a reputation as a hell-raising heartbreaker who used and abused women, which she'd always thought rather exciting in a Neolithic way, but had yet to see any evidence.

'Cal!' Finlay called him over, and he turned away from the pretty journalist without a farewell, leaving her dark-faced with disappointment. 'You got a cigarette?'

'You know I've quit, wee bree,' he muttered, settling in beside his brother, although there was far more room beside Lydia. He looked at her with cool, appraising eyes – smaller and colder than Finlay's, with short stubby blond lashes rather than his brother's long, sooty ones. They were the same shade of silver-grey, but whereas Finlay's danced like dolphin's backs through surf, Calum's were still and dark as a stingray lying on the bottom of the ocean. Accustomed to men fawning, Lydia was somehow certain he disapproved of her.

'I'll go and buy some, then.' Finlay ambled off in search of the tobacco girl, leaving Lydia alone with his stingray-eyed sibling. She flashed him her most ravishing smile but he didn't reciprocate.

'You not known my bree long, then?' Calum asked.

'Oh, ages – we used to work together,' Lydia noticed his accent was far thicker than Finlay's, 'but Fin's just junked in his job.'

'He was fired,' Calum corrected matter-of-factly.

'Same thing, darling.' The specifics didn't bother Lydia. She gave him another big smile. 'I'm leaving, too. We want to explore other avenues. I'm going to be a sex therapist.'

Not one flicker of surprise crossed Calum's watchful, bony face. He barely seemed interested. 'And Finlay?'

'Still deciding.' Lydia started repeating her spiel about how fashionable it was, opting out of a safe career. Calum said nothing, although his eyes still bored into her face with their unsettling, level gaze. Lydia couldn't resist backing up her argument. 'Odette's doing it too, you know.'

'Odette?' Calum didn't appear to recognise the name.

'Fielding – she introduced us earlier. Don't be misled by the eighties shoulderpads and the Cockney accent. She's one of the sharpest operators in the business – she can work a room like a pick-pocket.' Lydia liked the sound of that although she wasn't certain it reflected well on her friend. Now that Finlay was out of earshot, she could afford to lavish some praise. 'She wants to start a restaurant.'

'I remember – good concept, wrong location,' Calum muttered irritably. 'There are too many fucking restaurants in London already. I'm bored of London. We all are.'

'Oh, I agree!' Lydia was determined to get him to like her. He was practically family after all. 'Cool Britannia's so out of date. That's why London needs an injection of something new and original. Odette has such a clever mind, such a feeling for public opinion, that she can tell you what everyone will want next week, next year, next decade – and sell it to them. I haven't known her that long – we met through my friend Joo – but already I can tell she's going to be one of my best, best friends. We have the same attitude to sex. We absolutely adore it.'

'Is that a fact?' Calum twisted up the side of his mouth,

clearly wondering if Lydia was playing some sort of demented Cupid role. If she was, then she was way off-beam.

Lydia nodded, on something of a roll. 'Speak of the devil – Odette! Darling, over here!'

Having sent the pissed Meat Council man packing in a taxi before he could try to make a third unwanted pass at her, Odette was about to leave herself. Reluctantly, she walked over to Lydia's table, eyeing Calum who was looking extraordinarily uncomfortable.

'Calum and I have just been talking about your restaurant,' Lydia announced brightly.

'For fuck's sake, keep your voice down.' Odette was too annoyed to be polite.

Looking deeply hurt, Lydia played with the tassels on her trendy crocheted poncho.

'Sorry, babes.' Odette sat down beside her. 'It's just I'm still doing the day job, y'know?'

'Sure.' Lydia pursed her lips.

'And Calum's already said he wasn't interested.' She shot him a sympathetic look, bearing no particular grudge. The decision was his to make. It was she who'd blown it, after all.

'Now who on earth said that?' Calum looked at her levelly.

Odette watched his face for a moment, her heart hammering delightedly in her chest, suddenly drinking in the familiar rush of adrenalin which drenched her body when she spotted a buying signal. But before she could work out the best way of dealing with Calum's straight-faced volte face, Lydia pitched in with what she thought to be a selling line.

'I think you two would be perfect together! You'd make such a good double act, like Dempsey and Makepeace, Sapphire and Steel, Jonathan and Jennifer Hart.'

'What did you say?' Odette felt her blush crack right through her makeup this time and steam its way up her face.

'Oh, you must invest, Calum.' Lydia ignored her and stared at her almost-lover's brother with imploring eyes, as huge and blue as two second-class stamps. 'It makes so much sense. Odette is a genius.'

'I don't deny the project interested me.' Calum finally spoke in a terse undertone. 'But I'm no' really in the market for another London restaurant right now. In fact I—'

'Don't be silly!' Lydia interrupted, hating his dampening tone. 'London just needs some new ideas.' She put a comforting hand on his leg and he flinched. 'We all feel drained and uninspired from time to time. What you need is fresh eyes. Lovely blue ones,' she breathed seductively, meaning Odette's, but batting her own huge cobalt peepers straight in his face.

Odette watched Calum with interest. He was clearly thrown by his brother's outlandishly flirtatious new girlfriend, his characteristic cool replaced by embarrassed confusion. The stumpy lady-killer was stumped for once. If he'd known Lydia better, as Odette did, he would know that she flirted with absolutely everyone.

'How are you doing, Odie?' Finlay slumped back on to the bench seat and unwrapped a fresh packet of Marlboro Light.

'Fine, babes.' Odette tried not to show the fact she disliked being called Odie even by her close friends, let alone someone she hardly knew.

'I'm trying to persuade your brother to become Odette's sleeping partner.' Lydia took hold of Finlay's hand just as he was about to light the long-awaited cigarette.

Finlay snorted. 'I thought you said Odie's going out with a gangland mobster called Beerbelly?' he asked Lydia, unlit cigarette bobbing in his mouth.

'I'm not talking about *that* sort of partner – not like us later tonight,' Lydia laughed, taking his cigarette and throwing it over her shoulder before drawing him into a long, sensual kiss.

Odette's blush deepened, but to her astonishment Calum looked at her intently. 'You have gangland connections?' He studied her thoughtfully.

'Sort of.' Odette decided her brother-in-law Craig qualified, albeit tenuously. And her very brief encounter with Barfly just about counted. Anything that impressed Calum could only be to her benefit right now, however humiliating.

'Well, I never,' he laughed. 'You shouldae said. This puts a very different perspective on things.'

'Why?' She was ruffled. 'I ain't using any of my contacts in my professional life.' Particularly when they only amounted to an in-law who resprayed stolen cars and a snog with a man who occasionally worked as a bailiff's heavy.

'Sure, sure.' He eyed her chest and to her hot-faced shame, Odette realised she could almost feel his eyes like sensual fingers on her skin. She stared fixedly at Finlay's cigarette, which had landed in a champagne flute. What was happening to her? She'd started to fancy Calum Forrester of all people.

'So, you two going to get it together?' Lydia asked, emerging breathlessly from her kiss.

Finlay started to giggle and Odette shot him a dirty look. 'She means do some business together. Not funny business.'

'All business is funny business.' Calum smiled into her eyes. Having now regained his sang-froid, he looked at Lydia and winked. 'Isn't it, beautiful?'

'So you'll agree to help Odie for me?' Lydia's slow, easy smile was so sexy Odette half-expected steam to come out of Calum's ears. She looked worriedly at Finlay, but he was just smiling inanely and puffing on a cigarette at last.

Then, to her surprise, Calum turned back to her, grasped her hand and pressed it hard to his lips. She could feel his stubble on her knuckles, teeth against her flesh, tongue grazing her skin. And something involuntary kicked deep inside her as two pale grey eyes looked up at her, or more specifically at her boobs.

'I think Lydia's right. We'll make a great team. We both like to get what we want.' He let her hand go.

'And you want to be a part of the best restaurant club to open in North London this century?' Odette grinned, slightly thrown by his unconventional approach but nonetheless thrilled.

'Oh, I want a little bit more than that, sister.' He winked.

'I'm not a nun,' Odette snorted, confused by 'sister'.

'So I gather.' Calum laughed dirtily.

Before Odette could protest, Finlay explained, 'Cal calls all women "sister".'

'Let's get champagne!' Lydia shrieked, delighted by her matchmaking. 'We have to celebrate. Then you and I are going home,' she growled at Finlay who went pale but allowed himself to be dragged to the bar to help collect the Krug.

18

As Odette escaped to the loo to powder her face, Calum lounged back into his seat with a degree of satisfaction. 'All women are sisters,' he breathed his favourite saying, 'except the ones you desire. They're beautiful.'

'What was that?' Lydia laughed as she brought back four glasses.

'I said, well done, beautiful.' Calum winked again. 'So you're happy I'm helping out your best, best friend then?' He mocked her schoolgirl description.

'Oh, yes.' Lydia bent down to kiss him on the cheek, plunging him into the warm miasma of scent and hot skin rising from her top. 'I know Odette will love me for this.'

'She's not the only one,' Calum breathed, taking the champagne bottle.

Looking at her reflection in the mirror, Odette knew exactly who she could love. Amazing that Lydia had seen it and not her. She'd even said it: Dempsey and Makepeace, Sapphire and Steel, Jonathan and Jennifer. Odette was an eighties TV junkie and she felt as though she was about to star in her own series – *Fielding and Forrester*. Even their names sounded great together.

'You are going to open the best restaurant ever,' she told her reflection, not caring if talking to a mirror was a cranky eighties self-motivation trick; it worked for her. Closing her eyes, she added, 'And Calum Forrester is going to fall in love with you.'

Main Course

Main Course

1

Odette wasn't sure whether Vernon Dent was saying her name, or just muttering 'Oh, debt. Oh, debt. Oh, debt' over and over again under his breath.

He had been her bank manager for twelve years, ever since she'd opened her first current account in his Leytonstone High Street branch when enrolling as a student in the nearby London University college, Queen's. 'What are we going to do with you, my dear girl? You have released every asset that you had.' He brushed a plump, pink hand across the very few hairs spanning his pate. 'And you are indebted to us for quite a considerable loan, which as you know is secured against your property. We simply cannot offer you any more funds without equivalent collateral. Is there anything you can offer us as security? A car, perhaps?'

Odette thought about it. She thought about her beloved M3 Beamer, as fast as a ball bearing on oiled zinc. It had been a company car in which she'd squealed around the tight corners of her office's underground car park for the last time shortly after she'd junked in her job there. She'd officially been expected to work three months' notice, but they'd let her go early, encouraging her to chase her dream. The next day, she'd gone out and bought a brand new retro Vespa moped in turquoise metallic. Her friends had laughed, but she adored it and pointed out that it was immensely practical within the five square miles of London that she largely inhabited – Highbury, Islington, the West End and Stepney, where her parents lived.

'No, I haven't got a car no more, Vern – I mean Vernon.'

'I was hoping your business partner, Mr . . . er . . .' he checked his notes '. . . Mr Forrester would be here?'

'He's busy,' Odette bluffed.

'Well, I would really like to meet him face-to-face at some point. He has, after all, invested very heavily in this venture. Very heavily indeed. I must say I'm surprised he's not taking a more active interest at this stage.'

Not nearly so surprised as me, Odette thought darkly, trying to keep her smile even as she stared Vernon out, desperate to reassure him. 'Oh, Calum is interested – very interested, and hugely supportive. I keep him regularly informed. But as you may have read in the papers, he prefers to stay in the background when it comes to his restaurant empire.'

'I'd hardly say that,' Vernon chuckled, fishing his *Daily Mail* out of his briefcase and turning to the diary page where Calum was yet again featured in a small photograph with Robbie Williams, Eddie Irvine and a brace of blondes.

'I meant on the business front.' Odette's jaw tightened with the strain of smiling.

'Leave it with me, Odette dear.' Vernon mustered a weary, lop-sided smile. 'I think I may be able to arrange a further five thousand.'

'Five thousand?' Odette winced. She needed ten times that to get the OD open in time. She had less than a fortnight to go, and the builders were two weeks behind their much-revised schedule.

'I'll see what I can do. We'll talk on Monday,' he promised, pumping her hand in his – a familiar experience, something akin to getting one's hand stuck down the back of the sofa while groping for coins. But Odette needed far more than loose change right now – and a measly five K was going to rattle loudly in the old fire station she intended to transform into the trendiest media haunt in London. The place was burning up money and there were no longer any fire fighters around to put out the blaze. Odette knew she'd have to stand a lot more heat before she could get out of the kitchens, and was happy to fight this fire. She only wished Calum were as willing.

At first Odette had thought his ideas for the new venture inspired, if far too ambitious. They had argued endlessly over design, scale, costs and theme. She'd enjoyed these fights – it was in her nature to negotiate fiercely, and Calum was a great sparring partner – but now she saw that time had galloped away with them, and nothing was getting done. Now that the project had changed scale to fit in with Calum's plans, it was impossible to make progress without his say-so – or rather his cash. The impressive crew he had promised to replace her original line-up had yet to materialise. What was most worrying was that the publicity and marketing for the opening night – something Odette had wanted to handle herself – were on hold because Calum had insisted that with his contacts he could do it better. Major decisions were still hanging in the air like the unused pots and pans hanging from hooks in the OD kitchens, and arguments lay unfinished like the components of the huge OD bar.

Calum wanted high-gothic religion, Odette wanted minimalist drug-culture; Calum wanted a members-only bar and private rooms, Odette wanted a busy basement bar and a cabaret club with famous singers and comics entertaining a small crowd in thirties Berlin-style intimacy. She had hired her friend Juno to be the maître emcee; Calum had told her to fire her. He wanted the OD to open on a far grander scale than Odette, who had always planned to start small and expand into the space, to hire trusted friends and work in a tight group. Calum insisted that it was vital to keep a distance between employer and staff. Lately this distance had also been from kept from Odette.

Calum was legendary for going out on the town every night with his mob of media-star friends. Every hip journalist, DJ, footballer, artist, pop star, actor and PR supremo wanted to be his mate. For a thin, ugly Glaswegian who wore flower-pot hats, orange-tinted glasses with thick black rims, football shirts, baggy jogging bottoms and seventies trainers, he was bizarrely popular. And he was also the most unprofessional businessman Odette had ever met, as his drunken change of heart at Wayne Street's book launch had proven. His initial investment in the OD had been handed to her in a brown envelope: thirty thousand pounds in dirty red fifties. Odette had insisted on hiring an accountant, at which Calum had merely shrugged his shoulders and said, 'If you must.' He regularly forgot meetings, called her in the early hours, arranged to meet in noisy bars and clubs, lost vital pieces of paper, sent strange friends in his place and changed his mind about things without telling her. Odette knew that he was one of the most successful club owners and promoters in London, but she had no idea why. All he seemed to do was delight in winding her up. He had effectively thrown out her original proposal and was now toying with his own ideas, like a child inheriting a Lego set and claiming it for himself.

They were supposed to be meeting that afternoon to discuss the financial crisis, but Odette hadn't been able to contact him all week to arrange a time. Calum had no office as such, and refused to own a mobile phone. As co-founder of the famous Nero Club, he was occasionally found there; often he'd hang out at Desk, the super-trendy conceptual restaurant which he co-owned; he had an office in the cult night-club Therapy, but he rarely used it because he disliked the bar manager so much; sometimes he worked from his newest Dean Street restaurant and bar, the Clinic; at other times he could be tracked down at Office Block, that trendiest of all private members' clubs in Soho where he had sealed his commitment to the OD with a kiss on Odette's hand. He seemed to like the joke that when asked where he would be on any given day he could answer 'At my Desk' or 'The Office Block as usual' or 'At the Clinic and then on to Therapy'. Today he was at none of them. Odette tried each one in turn as she belted around London on the Vespa feeling like Penelope Pittstop on a mission.

She found Calum more confusing than ever. He seemed to have grown bored with the OD recently and that terrified her far more than his over-budget ideas; he hadn't even visited the old fire station in Islington for more than a month. Meanwhile she had read in yesterday's *Evening Standard* that he was rumoured to be looking for a restaurant venue in Brighton. He was supposed to be co-partner with equal input, but he was proving to be a sleeping partner who played with other people between the balance sheets.

Calum had initially promised the two trendiest artists in town, the Leonard brothers, Jed and Jago, to create her interior – not camp Maurice Lloyd-Brewster, a design specialist obsessed with loos. Calum's kitchen designer had insisted on

Contents

Illustrations

The *VOYAGES of*
DOCTOR DOLITTLE

PROLOGUE

ALL that I have written so far about Doctor Dolittle I heard long after it happened from those who had known him — indeed a great deal of it took place before I was born. But I now come to set down that part of the great man's life which I myself saw and took part in.

Many years ago the Doctor gave me permission to do this. But we were both of us so busy then voyaging around the world, having adventures and filling notebooks full of natural history that I never seemed to get time to sit down and write of our doings.

Now, of course, when I am quite an old man, my memory isn't so good any more. But whenever I am in doubt and have to hesitate and think, I always ask Polynesia, the parrot.

That wonderful bird (she is now nearly two hundred and fifty years old) sits on the top of my desk, usually humming sailor songs to herself while I write this book. And, as everyone who ever met her knows, Polynesia's memory is the most marvellous memory in the world.

First of all, I must tell you something about myself and how I came to meet the Doctor.

PART I

'I would sit on the river wall with my feet dangling
over the water'

Chapter One
THE COBBLER'S SON

MY name is Tommy Stubbins, son of Jacob Stubbins, the cobbler of Puddleby-on-the-Marsh; I was nine and a half years old. At that time Puddleby was only quite a small town. A river ran through the middle of it, and over this river there was a very old stone bridge called Kingsbridge, which led you from the market place on one side to the churchyard on the other.

Sailing ships came up this river from the sea and anchored near the bridge. I used to go down and watch the sailors unloading the ships upon the river wall. The sailors sang strange songs as they pulled upon the ropes, and I learned these songs by heart. And I would sit on the river wall with my feet dangling over the water and sing with the men, pretending to myself that I, too, was a sailor.

For I longed always to sail away with those brave ships when they turned their backs on Puddleby Church and went creeping down the river again, across the wide, lonely marshes to the sea. I longed to go with them out into the world to seek my fortune in foreign lands – Africa, India, China, and Peru! When they got round the bend in the river and the water was hidden from view, you could still see their huge brown sails towering over the roofs of the town, moving onward slowly – like some gentle giants that walked among the houses without noise. What strange things would they have seen, I wondered, when next they came back to anchor at Kingsbridge! And, dreaming of the lands I had never seen, I'd sit on there, watching till they were out of sight.

Three great friends I had in Puddleby in those days. One was Joe, the mussel man, who lived in a tiny hut by the edge of the water under the bridge. This old man was simply marvellous at making things. I never saw a man so clever with his hands. He used to mend my toy ships for me, which

I sailed upon the river; he built windmills out of packing cases and barrel staves, and he could make the most wonderful kites from old umbrellas.

Joe would sometimes take me in his mussel boat, and when the tide was running out we would paddle down the river as far as the edge of the sea to get mussels and lobsters to sell. And out there on the cold, lonely marshes we would see wild geese flying, and curlews and redshanks and many other kinds of seabirds that live among the samphire and the long grass of the great salt fen. And as we crept up the river in the evening when the tide had turned, we would see the lights on Kingsbridge twinkle in the dusk, reminding us of tea time and warm fires.

Another friend I had was Matthew Mugg, the cat's-meat man. He was a funny old person with a bad squint. He looked rather awful, but he was really quite nice to talk to. He knew everybody in Puddleby, and he knew all the dogs and all the cats. In those times, being a cat's-meat man was a regular business. And you could see one nearly any day going through the streets with a wooden tray full of pieces of meat stuck on skewers crying, 'Meat! M-E-A-T!' People paid him to give this meat to their cats and dogs instead of feeding them on dog biscuits or the scraps from the table.

I enjoyed going round with old Matthew and seeing the cats and dogs come running to the garden gates whenever they heard his call. Sometimes he let me give the meat to the animals myself, and I thought this was great fun. He knew a lot about dogs and he would tell me the names of the different kinds as we went through the town. He had several dogs of his own; one, a whippet, was a very fast runner, and Matthew used to win prizes with her at the Saturday coursing races; another, a terrier, was a fine ratter. The cat's-meat man used to make a business of rat-catching for the millers and farmers as well as his other trade of selling cat's meat.

My third great friend was Luke the Hermit. But of him I will tell you more later on.

I did not go to school, because my father was not rich enough to send me. But I was extremely fond of animals. So I used to spend my time collecting birds' eggs and butterflies, fishing in the river, rambling through the countryside after blackberries and mushrooms, and helping the mussel man mend his nets.

Yes, it was a very pleasant life I lived in those days long ago – though of course I did not think so then. I was nine and a half years old, and, like all boys, I wanted to grow up – not knowing how well off I was with no cares and nothing to worry me. Always I longed for the time when I should be allowed to leave my father's house, to take passage in one of those brave ships, to sail down the river through the misty marshes to the sea – out into the world to seek my fortune.

Chapter Two
I HEAR OF THE GREAT NATURALIST

ONE early morning in the spring-time, when I was wandering among the hills at the back of the town, I happened to come upon a hawk with a squirrel in its claws. It was standing on a rock, and the squirrel was fighting very hard for its life. The hawk was so frightened when I came upon it suddenly like this, that it dropped the poor creature and flew away. I picked the squirrel up and found that two of its legs were badly hurt. So I carried it in my arms back to the town.

When I came to the bridge I went into the mussel man's hut and asked him if he could do anything for it. Joe put on his spectacles and examined it carefully. Then he shook his head.

'I came upon a hawk with a squirrel in its claws'

'Yon crittur's got a broken leg,' he said, 'and another badly cut an' all. I can mend you your boats, Tom, but I haven't the tools nor the learning to make a broken squirrel seaworthy. This is a job for a surgeon — and for a right smart one an' all. There be only one man I know who could save yon crittur's life. And that's John Dolittle.'

'Who is John Dolittle?' I asked. 'Is he a vet?'

'No,' said the mussel man. 'He's no vet. Doctor Dolittle is a nacheralist.'

'What's a nacheralist?'

'A nacheralist,' said Joe, putting away his glasses and starting to fill his pipe, 'is a person who knows all about animals and butterflies and plants and rocks an' all. John Dolittle is a very great nacheralist. I'm surprised you never heard of him – and you daft over animals. He knows a whole lot about shellfish – that I know from my own knowledge. He's a quiet man and don't talk much, but there's folks who do say he's the greatest nacheralist in the world.'

'Where does he live?' I asked.

'Over on the Oxenthorpe Road, t'other side the town. Don't know just which house it is, but 'most anyone 'cross there could tell you, I reckon. Go and see him. He's a great man.'

So I thanked the mussel man, took up my squirrel again and started off towards the Oxenthorpe Road.

The first thing I heard as I came into the market place was someone calling 'Meat! M-E-A-T!'

'There's Matthew Mugg,' I said to myself. 'He'll know where this Doctor lives. Matthew knows everyone.'

So I hurried across the market place and caught up with him.

'Matthew,' I said, 'do you know Doctor Dolittle?'

'Do I know John Dolittle!' said he. 'Well, I should think I do! I know him as well as I know my own wife – better, I sometimes think. He's a great man – a very great man.'

'Can you show me where he lives?' I asked. 'I want to take this squirrel to him. It has a broken leg.'

'Certainly,' said the cat's-meat man. 'I'll be going right by his house directly. Come along and I'll show you.'

So off we went together.

'Oh, I've known John Dolittle for years and years,' said Matthew as we made our way out of the market place. 'But I'm pretty sure he ain't home just now. He's away on a voyage. But he's liable to be back any day. I'll show you his house and then you'll know where to find him.'

All the way down the Oxenthorpe Road, Matthew hardly stopped talking about his great friend John Dolittle . . . "M.D." He talked so much that he forgot all about calling out 'Meat!' until we both suddenly noticed that we had a whole procession of dogs following us patiently.

'Where did the Doctor go to on this voyage?' I asked as Matthew handed round the meat to them.

'I couldn't tell you,' he answered. 'Nobody never knows where he goes, nor when he's going, nor when he's coming back. He lives all alone except for his pets. He's made some great voyages and some wonderful discoveries. Last time he came back he told me he'd found a tribe of Indians in the Pacific Ocean — lived on two islands, they did. The husbands lived on one island and the wives lived on the other. Sensible people, some of them Indians. They met only once a year, when the husbands came over to visit the wives for a great feast — Christmas-time, most likely. Yes, he's a wonderful man is the Doctor. And as for animals, well, there ain't no one knows as much about 'em as what he does.'

'How did he get to know so much about animals?' I asked.

The cat's-meat man stopped and leaned down to whisper in my ear.

He talks their language, he said in a hoarse, mysterious voice.

'The animals' language?' I cried.

'Why, certainly,' said Matthew. 'All animals have some kind of language. Some sorts talk more than others; some speak only in sign language. But the Doctor, he understands them all – birds as well as animals. We keep it a secret though, him and me, because folks only laugh at you when you speak of it. Why, he can even write animal language. He reads aloud to his pets. He's wrote history books in monkey talk, poetry in canary language, and comic songs for magpies to sing. It's a fact. He's now busy learning the language of the shellfish. But he says it's hard work – and he has caught some terrible colds, holding his head under water so much. He's a great man.'

'He certainly must be,' I said. 'I do wish he were home so I could meet him.'

'Well, there's) is house,' said the cat's-meat man. 'Look, that little one at the bend of the road there – the one high up – like it was sitting on the wall above the street.'

We were now come beyond the edge of the town. And the house that Matthew pointed out was quite a small one standing by itself. There seemed to be a big garden around it;

and this garden was much higher than the road, so you had to go up a flight of steps in the wall before you reached the front gate at the top. I could see that there were many fine fruit trees in the garden, for their branches hung down over the wall in places. But the wall was so high I could not see anything else.

When we reached the house Matthew went up the steps to the front gate and I followed him. I thought he was going to go into the garden, but the gate was locked. A dog came running down from the house and he took several pieces of meat, which the cat's-meat man pushed through the bars of the gate, and some paper bags full of corn and bran. I noticed that this dog did not stop to eat the meat, as any ordinary dog would have done, but he took all the things back to the house and disappeared. He had a curious wide collar round his neck that looked as though it were made of brass or something. Then we came away.

'The Doctor isn't back yet,' said Matthew, 'or the gate wouldn't be locked.'

'What were all those things in paper bags you gave the dog?' I asked.

'Oh, those were provisions,' said Matthew,

'things for the animals to eat. The Doctor's house is simply full of pets. I give the things to the dog while the Doctor's away, and the dog gives them to the other animals.'

'And what was that curious collar he was wearing round his neck?'

'That's a solid gold dog collar,' said Matthew. 'It was given to him when he was with the Doctor on one of his voyages long ago. He saved a man's life.'

'How long has the Doctor had him?' I asked.

'Oh, a long time. Jip's getting pretty old now. That's why the Doctor doesn't take him on his voyages any more. He leaves him behind to take care of the house. Every Monday and Thursday I bring the food to the gate here and give it him through the bars. He never lets anyone come inside the garden while the Doctor's away – not even me, though he knows me well. But you'll always be able to tell if the Doctor's back or not – because if he is, the gate will surely be open.'

So I went off home to my father's house and put my squirrel to bed in an old wooden box full of straw. And there I nursed him myself and took care of him as best I could till the time should come when the Doctor would return. And every day I went to the little house with the big garden on the edge of the town and tried the gate to see if it was locked. Sometimes the dog, Jip, would come down to the gate to meet me. But though he always wagged his tail and seemed glad to see me, he never let me come inside the garden.

Chapter Three
THE DOCTOR'S HOME

ONE Monday afternoon towards the end of April my father asked me to take some shoes that he had mended to a house on the other side of the town. They were for a Colonel Bellowes, who was very particular.

I found the house and rang the bell at the front door. The Colonel opened it, stuck out a very red face, and said, 'Go around to the tradesmen's entrance – go to the back door.' Then he slammed the door shut.

I felt inclined to throw the shoes into the middle of his flower bed. But I thought my father might be angry, so I didn't. I went round to the back door, and there the Colonel's wife met me and took the shoes from me. She seemed to be terribly afraid of her husband, whom I could still hear stumping around the house somewhere, grunting indignantly because I had come to the front door. Then she asked me in a whisper if I would have a bun and a glass of milk. And I said. 'Yes, please.'

After I had eaten the bun and milk and thanked the Colonel's wife, I thought that I would see if the Doctor had come back yet. My squirrel wasn't getting any better, and I was beginning to be worried about him.

So I started off toward the Doctor's house. On the way I noticed that the sky was clouding over and that it looked as though it might rain.

I reached the gate and found it locked. I felt very discouraged. I had been coming here every day for a week now. The dog, Jip, came to the gate and wagged his tail as usual, and then sat down and watched me closely to see that I didn't get in.

I began to fear that my squirrel would die before the Doctor came back. I turned away sadly, went down the steps on to the road, and turned towards home again.

I wondered if it was supper-time yet. Of course I had no watch of my own, but I noticed a gentleman coming towards me down the road; and when he got nearer, I saw it was the Colonel out for a walk. He was all wrapped up in smart overcoats and mufflers and bright-coloured gloves. It was not a very cold day, but he had so many clothes on he looked like a pillow inside a roll of blankets. I asked him if he would please tell me the time.

He stopped, grunted, and glared down at me – his red face growing redder still; and when he spoke it sounded like the cork coming out of a gingerbeer bottle.

'Do you imagine for one moment,' he spluttered, 'that I am going to get myself all unbuttoned just to tell a little boy like you *the time*!' And he went stumping down the street grunting harder than ever.

I stood still a moment looking after him and wondering how old I would have to be to have him go to the trouble of getting his watch out. And then, all of a sudden, the rain came down in torrents.

I have never seen it rain so hard. It got dark, almost like night. The wind began to blow; the thunder rolled; the lightning flashed; and in a moment, the gutters of the road were flowing like a river. There was no place handy to take shelter, so I put my head down against the driving wind and started to run towards home.

I hadn't gone very far when my head bumped into something soft, and I sat down suddenly on the pavement. I looked up to see whom I had run into. And there in front of me, sitting on the wet pavement like myself, was a little round man with a very kind face. He wore a shabby high hat and in his hand he had a small black bag.

'I'm very sorry,' I said. 'I had my head down and I didn't see you coming.'

To my great surprise, instead of getting angry at being knocked down, the little man began to laugh.

'It was just as much my fault as it was yours, you know,' said the little man. 'I had my head down too — but look here we mustn't sit talking like this. You must be soaked. I know I am. How far have you got to go?'

'My home is on the other side of the town,' I said as we picked ourselves up.

'My goodness, but that *was* a wet pavement!' said he. 'And, I declare, it's coming down worse than ever. Come along to my house and get dried. A storm like this can't last.'

He took hold of my hand and we started

running back down the road together. As we ran I began to wonder who this funny little man could be and where he lived. I was a perfect stranger to him, and yet he was taking me to his own home to get dried. Such a change, after the old red-faced Colonel who had refused even to tell me the time! Presently we stopped.

'Here we are,' he said.

I looked up to see where we were and found myself back at the foot of the steps leading to the little house with the big garden! My new friend was already running up the steps and opening the gate with some keys he took from his pocket.

Surely, I thought, this cannot be the great Doctor Dolittle himself!

I suppose after hearing so much about him I had expected someone very tall and strong and marvellous. It was hard to believe that this funny little man with the kind smiling face could really be he. Yet here he was, opening the very gate which I had been watching for so many days!

The dog, Jip, came rushing out and started jumping up on him and barking with happiness. The rain was splashing down heavier then ever.

'Are you Doctor Dolittle?' I shouted as we sped up the short garden path to the house.

'Yes, I'm Doctor Dolittle,' said he, opening the front door with the same bunch of keys. 'Get in! Don't bother about wiping your feet. Never mind the mud. Take it in with you. Get in out of the rain!'

I popped in, he and Jip following. Then he slammed the door to behind us.

The storm had made it dark enough outside, but inside the house, with the door closed, it was as black as night. Then began the most extraordinary noise that I have ever heard. It sounded like all sorts and kinds of animals and birds calling and squeaking and screeching at the same time. I could hear things trundling down the stairs and hurrying along passages. Somewhere in the dark a duck was quacking, a cock was crowing, a dove was cooing, an owl was hooting, a lamb was bleating, and Jip was barking. I felt birds' wings fluttering and fanning near my face. Things kept bumping into my legs and nearly upsetting me. The whole front hall seemed to be filling up with animals. The noise, together with the roaring of the rain, was tremendous; and I was beginning to grow a little bit scared when I felt the Doctor take hold of my arm and shout into my ear.

'Don't be alarmed. Don't be frightened. These are just some of my pets. I've been away three months and they are glad to see me home again. Stand still where you are till I strike a light. My gracious, what a storm! Just listen to that thunder!'

So there I stood in the pitch-black dark, while all kinds of animals that I couldn't see chattered and jostled around me. It all seemed like some queer dream and I was beginning to wonder if I was really awake, when I heard the Doctor speaking again: 'My blessed matches are all wet. They won't strike. Have you got any?'

'No, I'm afraid I haven't,' I called back.

'Never mind,' said he. 'Perhaps Dab-Dab can raise us a light somewhere.'

Then the Doctor made some funny clicking noises with his tongue and I heard someone trundle up the stairs again and start moving about in the rooms above.

Then we waited quite a while without anything happening.

'Will the light be long in coming?' I asked. 'Some animal is sitting on my foot and my toes are going to sleep.'

'No, only a minute,' said the Doctor. 'She'll be back in a minute.'

And just then I saw the first glimmerings of a light around the landing above. At once all the animals kept quiet.

'I thought you lived alone,' I said to the Doctor.

'So I do,' said he. 'It is Dab-Dab who is bringing the light.' I looked up the stairs trying to make out who was coming. I could not see around the landing, but I heard the most curious footstep on the upper flight. It sounded like someone hopping down from one step to the other, as though he were using only one leg.

As the light came lower, it grew brighter and began to throw strange jumping shadows on the walls.

'Ah – at last!' said the Doctor. 'Good old Dab-Dab!'

And then I thought I *really* must be dreaming. For there, craning her neck round the bend of the landing, hopping down the stairs on one leg, came a spotless white duck. And in her right foot she carried a lighted candle!

'And in her right foot she carried a lighted candle!'

Chapter Four
THE WIFF-WAFF

WHEN at last I could look around me I found that the hall was indeed simply full of animals. It seemed to me that almost every kind of creature from the countryside must be there: a pigeon, a white rat, an owl, a badger, a jackdaw – there was even a small pig, just in from the rainy garden, carefully wiping his feet on the mat while the light from the candle glistened on his wet pink back.

The Doctor took the candlestick from the duck and turned to me.

'Look here,' he said, 'you must get those wet clothes off – by the way, what is your name?'

'Tommy Stubbins,' I said.

'Oh, are you the son of Jacob Stubbins, the shoemaker?'

'Yes,' I said.

'Excellent bootmaker, your father,' said the Doctor. 'You see these?' and he held up his right foot to show me the enormous boots he was wearing. 'Your father made those boots four years ago, and I've been wearing them ever since – perfectly wonderful boots. Well now, look here, Stubbins, you've got to change those wet things – and quick. Wait a moment till I get some more candles lit, and then we'll go upstairs and find some dry clothes. You'll have to wear an old suit of mine till we can get yours dry again by the kitchen fire.'

So presently when more candles had been lighted round different parts of the house, we went upstairs; and when we had come into a bedroom the Doctor opened a big wardrobe and took out two suits of old clothes. These we put on. Then we carried our wet ones down to the kitchen and started a fire in the big chimney. The coat of the Doctor's that I was wearing was so large for me that I kept treading on my own coat-tails while I was helping to fetch the wood up from the cellar. But very soon we had a huge big fire blazing up the chimney and we hung our wet clothes around on chairs.

'Now let's cook some supper,' said the Doctor. 'You'll stay and have supper with me, Stubbins, of course?'

Already I was beginning to be very fond of this funny little man who called me 'Stubbins' instead of 'Tommy' or 'little lad' (I did so hate to be called 'little lad'!). This man seemed to begin right away treating me as though I were a grown-up friend of his. And when he asked me to stop and have supper with him I felt terribly proud and happy. But I suddenly remembered that I had not told my mother that I would be out late. So very sadly I answered, 'Thank you very much. I would like to stay, but I am afraid that my mother will begin to worry and wonder where I am if I don't get back.'

'Oh, but my dear Stubbins,' said the Doctor, throwing another log of wood on the fire, 'your clothes aren't dry yet. You'll have to wait for them, won't you? By the time they are ready to put on, we will have supper cooked and eaten. . . . Did you see where I put my bag?'

'I think it is still in the hall,' I said. 'I'll go and see.'

I found the bag near the front door. It was made of black leather and looked very, very old. One of its latches was broken and it was tied up around the middle with a piece of string.

'Thank you,' said the Doctor when I brought it to him.

'Was that bag all the luggage you had for your voyage?' I asked.

'Yes,' said the Doctor, as he undid the piece of string. 'I don't believe in a lot of baggage. It's such a nuisance. Life's too short to fuss with it. And it isn't really necessary, you know. . . . Where *did* I put those sausages?'

The Doctor was feeling about inside the bag. First he brought out a loaf of new bread. Next came a glass jar with a curious metal top to it. He held this up to the light very carefully before he set it down upon the table, and I could see that there was some strange little water-creature swimming about inside. At last the Doctor brought out a pound of sausages.

'Now,' he said, 'all we want is a frying pan.'

We went into the scullery and there we found some pots and pans hanging against the wall. The Doctor took down the frying pan.

While the Doctor was busy cooking I went

and took another look at the funny little
creature swimming about in the glass jar.

'What is this animal?' I asked.

'Oh that,' said the Doctor turning round,
'that's a Wiff-Waff. Its full name is *hip-
pocampus pippitopitus*. But the natives just
call it a Wiff-Waff – on account of the way
it waves its tail, swimming, I imagine.
That's what I went on this last voyage for, to
get that. You see I'm very busy just now
trying to learn the language of the shellfish.
They *have* language, of that I feel sure. I can
talk a little shark language and porpoise
dialect. But what I particularly want to
learn now is shellfish.'

'Why?' I asked.

'Well, you see, some of the shellfish are the
oldest kind of animals in the world that we
know of. We find their shells in the rocks –
turned to stone – thousands of years old. So
I feel quite sure that if I could only get to
talk their language, I should be able to learn
a whole lot about what the world was like
ages ago. You see?'

'But couldn't some of the other animals
tell you as well?'

'I don't think so,' said the Doctor, prodding
the sausages with a fork. 'To be sure, the

monkeys I knew in Africa some time ago were very helpful in telling me about bygone days, but they only went back a thousand years or so. No, I am certain that the oldest history in the world is to be had from the shellfish – and from them only. You see, most of the other animals that were alive in those ancient times have now become extinct.'

'Have you learned any shellfish language yet?' I asked.

'No. I've only just begun. I wanted this particular kind of a pipefish because he is half shellfish and half ordinary fish. I went all the way to the Eastern Mediterranean after him. But I'm very much afraid he isn't going to be a great deal of help to me. To tell you the truth, I'm rather disappointed in his appearance. He doesn't *look* very intelligent, does he?'

'No, he doesn't,' I agreed.

'Ah,' said the Doctor. 'The sausages are done to a turn. Come along – hold your plate near and let me give you some.'

Then we sat down at the kitchen table and started a hearty meal.

It was a wonderful kitchen, that. I had many meals there afterwards and I found it a better place to eat in than the grandest dining room in the world. It was so cosy and home-like and warm. It was so handy for the food too. You took it right off the fire, hot, and put it on the table and ate it. And you could watch your toast toasting at the fender and see it didn't burn while you drank your soup. And if you had forgotten to put the salt on the table, you didn't have to get up and go into another room to fetch it; you just reached around and took the big wooden box off the dresser behind you. Then the fireplace – the biggest fireplace you ever saw – was like a room in itself. You could get right inside it, even when the logs were burning, and sit on the wide seats either side and roast chestnuts after the meal was over – or listen to the kettle singing, or tell stories, or look at picture books by the light of the fire. It was a marvellous kitchen. It was like the Doctor, comfortable, sensible, friendly and solid.

While we were gobbling away, the door suddenly opened and in marched the duck, Dab-Dab and the dog, Jip, dragging sheets and pillowcases behind them over the clean tiled floor. The Doctor, seeing how surprised I was, explained: 'They're just going to air

the bedding for me in front of the fire. Dab-
Dab is a perfect treasure of a housekeeper;
she never forgets anything. I had a sister
once who used to keep house for me (poor,
dear Sarah! I wonder how she's getting on –
I haven't seen her in many years). But she
wasn't nearly as good as Dab-Dab. Have
another sausage?'

The Doctor turned and said a few words to
the dog and duck in some strange talk and
signs. They seemed to understand him
perfectly.

'Can you talk in squirrel language?' I
asked.

'Oh yes. That's quite an easy language,'
said the Doctor. 'You could learn that
yourself without a great deal of trouble. But
why do you ask?'

'Because I have a sick squirrel at home,' I
said. 'I took it away from a hawk. But two of
its legs are badly hurt and I wanted very
much to have you see it, if you would. Shall
I bring it tomorrow?'

'Well, if its leg is badly broken I think I
had better see it tonight. It may be too late
to do much, but I'll come home with you and
take a look at it.'

So presently we felt the clothes by the fire

and mine were found to be quite dry. I took them upstairs to the bedroom and changed, and when I came down the Doctor was all ready, waiting for me with his little black bag full of medicines and bandages.

'Come along,' he said. 'The rain has stopped now.'

Outside it had grown bright again and the evening sky was all red with the setting sun; and thrushes were singing in the garden as we opened the gate to go down on to the road.

Chapter Five
POLYNESIA

'I THINK your house is the most interesting house I was ever in,' I said as we set off in the direction of the town. 'May I come and see you again tomorrow?'

'Certainly,' said the Doctor. 'Come any day you like. Tomorrow I'll show you the garden and my private zoo.'

'Oh, have you a zoo?' I asked.

'Yes,' said he. 'The larger animals are too big for the house, so I keep them in a zoo in the garden. It is not a very big collection, but it is interesting in its way.'

'It must be splendid,' I said, 'to be able to talk all the languages of the different animals. Do you think I could ever learn to do it?'

'Oh surely,' said the Doctor, '. . . with

practice. You have to be very patient, you know. You really ought to have Polynesia to start you. It was she who gave me my first lessons.'

'Who is Polynesia?' I asked.

'Polynesia was a West African parrot I had. She isn't with me any more now,' said the Doctor sadly.

'Why? Is she dead?'

'Oh, no,' said the Doctor. 'She is still living, I hope. But when we reached Africa she seemed so glad to get back to her own country. She wept for joy. And when the time came for me to come back here I had not the heart to take her away from that sunny land – although, it is true, she did offer to come. I left her in Africa. Ah, well! I have missed her terribly. She wept again when we left. But I think I did the right thing. She was one of the best friends I ever had. It was she who first gave me the idea of learning the animal languages and becoming an animal doctor. I often wonder if she remained happy in Africa, and whether I shall ever see her funny old solemn face again. Good old Polynesia! A most extraordinary bird – well, well!'

Just at that moment we heard the noise of

someone running behind us and, turning round, we saw Jip, the dog, rushing down the road after us as fast as his legs could bring him. He seemed very excited about something, and as soon as he came up to us he started barking and whining to the Doctor in a peculiar way. Then the Doctor too seemed to get all worked up and began talking and making queer signs to the dog.

At length he turned to me, his face shining with happiness. 'Polynesia has come back!' he cried. 'Imagine it! Jip says she has just arrived at the house. My! And it's five years since I saw her. . . . excuse me a minute.'

He turned as if to go back home. But the parrot, Polynesia, was already flying towards us. The Doctor clapped his hands like a child getting a new toy, while the swarm of sparrows in the roadway fluttered, gossiping, up on to the fences, highly scandalized to see a grey and scarlet parrot skimming down an English lane.

On she came, straight on to the Doctor's shoulder, where she immediately began talking a steady stream in a language I could not understand. She seemed to have a terrible lot to say. And very soon the Doctor had forgotten all about me and my squirrel and Jip and everything else, till at length the bird clearly asked him something about me.

'Oh, excuse me, Stubbins!' said the Doctor. 'I was so interested listening to my old friend here. We must get on and see this squirrel of yours. . . . Polynesia, this is Thomas Stubbins.'

The parrot, on the Doctor's shoulder, nodded gravely toward me and then, to my great surprise, said quite plainly in English, 'How do you do? I remember the night you were born. It was a terribly cold winter. You were a very ugly baby.'

'Stubbins is anxious to learn animal language,' said the Doctor. 'I was just telling him about you and the lessons you gave me, when Jip ran up and told us you had arrived.'

'Well,' said the parrot, turning to me, 'I may have started the Doctor learning, but I never could have done even that if he hadn't first taught me to understand what *I* was saying when I spoke English. You see, many parrots can talk like a person, but very few of them understand what they are saying. They just say it because . . . well, because

they fancy it is smart or because they know
they will get crackers given them.'

By this time we had turned and were going
towards my home with Jip running in front
and Polynesia still perched on the Doctor's
shoulder. The bird chattered incessantly,
mostly about Africa, but now she spoke in
English out of politeness to me.

'How is Prince Bumpo getting on?' asked
the Doctor.

'Oh, I'm glad you asked me,' said Polynesia.
'I almost forgot to tell you. What do you
think? *Bumpo is in England!*'

'In England! You don't say!' cried the
Doctor. 'What on earth is he doing here?'

'His father, the king, sent him here to a
place called, er, Bullford, I think it was, to
study lessons.'

'Bullford . . . Bullford,' muttered the
Doctor. 'I never heard of the place . . . oh, you
mean Oxford.'

'Yes, that's the place — Oxford,' said
Polynesia. 'I knew it had cattle in it
somewhere. Oxford — that's the place he's
gone to.'

'Well, well,' murmured the Doctor. 'Fancy
Bumpo studying at Oxford. Well, well!'

'There were great doings in Jolliginki

when he left. He was scared to death to come. He was the first man from that country to go abroad. But his father made him come. He said that all the African kings were sending their sons to Oxford now. It was the fashion, and he would have to go. Poor Bumpo went off in tears – and everybody in the palace was crying too. You never heard such a hullabaloo.'

'And how is Chee-Chee getting on? Chee-Chee,' added the Doctor in explanation to me, 'was a pet monkey I had years ago. I left him, too, in Africa when I came away.'

'Well,' said Polynesia frowning, 'Chee-Chee is not entirely happy. I saw a good deal of him the last few years. He got dreadfully homesick for you and the house and the garden. It's funny, but I was just the same way myself. I just couldn't seem to settle down. Well, one night I made up my mind that I'd come back here and find you. So I hunted up old Chee-Chee and told him about it. He said he didn't blame me a bit – felt exactly the same way himself. Africa was so deadly quiet after the life we had with you. He missed the stories you used to tell us and the chats we used to have sitting around the kitchen fire on winter nights.

The animals out there were very nice to us, and all that. But somehow the dear, kind creatures seemed a bit stupid. Chee-Chee said he had noticed it too. But I suppose it wasn't they who had changed; it was we who were different. When I left, poor old Chee-Chee broke down and cried. He said he felt as though his only friend were leaving him – though, as you know, he has simply millions of relatives there. He said it didn't seem fair that I should have wings to fly over here any time I liked, and him with no way to follow me. But mark my words, I wouldn't be a bit surprised if he found a way to come – some day. He's a smart lad, is Chee-Chee.'

At this point we arrived at my home. My father's shop was closed and the shutters were up, but my mother was standing at the door looking down the street.

'Good evening, Mrs Stubbins,' said the Doctor. 'It is my fault your son is so late. I made him stay to supper while his clothes were drying. He was soaked to the skin and so was I. We ran into one another in the storm and I insisted on his coming into my house for shelter.'

'I was beginning to get worried about him,'

said my mother. 'I am thankful to you, sir, for looking after him so well and bringing him home.'

'Don't mention it, don't mention it,' said the Doctor. 'We have had a very interesting chat.'

'Who might it be that I have the honour of addressing?' asked my mother, staring at the grey parrot perched on the Doctor's shoulder.

'Oh, I'm John Dolittle. I daresay your husband will remember me. He made me some very excellent boots about four years ago. They really are splendid,' added the Doctor, gazing down at his feet with great satisfaction.

'The Doctor has come to cure my squirrel, Mother,' said I. 'He knows all about animals.'

'Oh, no,' said the Doctor, 'not all, Stubbins, not all about them by any means.'

'It is very kind of you to come so far to look after his pet,' said my mother. 'Tom is always bringing home strange creatures from the woods and fields.'

'Is he?' said the Doctor. 'Perhaps he will grow up to be a naturalist some day. Who knows?'

'Won't you come in?' asked my mother. 'The place is a little untidy because I haven't finished the spring cleaning yet. But there's a nice fire burning in the parlour.'

'Thank you!' said the Doctor. 'What a charming home you have!'

And after wiping his enormous boots very, very carefully on the mat, the great man passed into the house.

Chapter Six
THE WOUNDED SQUIRREL

INSIDE we found my father busy practising on the flute beside the fire. This he always did, every evening, after his work was over.

The Doctor immediately began talking to him about flutes and piccolos and bassoons, and presently my father said, 'Perhaps you perform upon the flute yourself, sir. Won't you play us a tune?'

'Well,' said the Doctor, 'it is a long time since I touched the instrument. But I would like to try. May I?'

Then the Doctor took the flute from my father and played and played and played. It was wonderful. My mother and father sat as still as statues, staring up at the ceiling as though they were in church; and even I, who didn't bother much about music except on the mouth organ – even I felt all sad and cold and creepy and wished I had been a better boy.

'Oh, I think that was just beautiful!' sighed my mother when at length the Doctor stopped.

'You are a great musician, sir,' said my father, 'a very great musician. Won't you please play us something else?'

'Why certainly,' said the Doctor '... oh, but look here, I've forgotten all about the squirrel.'

'I'll show him to you,' I said. 'He is upstairs in my room.' So I led the Doctor to my bedroom at the top of the house and showed him the squirrel in the packing case filled with straw.

The animal, who had always seemed very afraid of me – though I had tried hard to make him feel at home – sat up at once when the Doctor came into the room and started to chatter. The Doctor chattered back in the same way and the squirrel, when he was lifted up to have his leg examined, appeared to be rather pleased than frightened.

I held a candle while the Doctor tied the

leg up in what he called 'splints,' which he made out of matchsticks with his penknife.

'I think you will find that his leg will get better now in a very short time,' said the Doctor, closing up his bag. 'Don't let him run about for at least two weeks yet, but keep him in the open air and cover him up with dry leaves if the nights get cool. He tells me he is rather lonely here all by himself and is wondering how his wife and children are getting on. I have assured him you are a man to be trusted, and I will send a squirrel who lives in my garden to find out how his family is and to bring him news of them. He must be kept cheerful at all costs. Squirrels are naturally a very cheerful, active race. It is very hard for them to lie still doing nothing. But you needn't worry about him. He will be all right.'

Then we went back again to the parlour, and my mother and father kept him playing the flute till after ten o'clock.

I often look back upon that night long, long ago. And if I close my eyes and think hard, I can see the parlour just as it was then: a funny little man in coat-tails, with a round kind of face, playing away on the flute in front of the fire; my mother on one side of him and my father on the other, holding their breath and listening with their eyes shut; myself, with Jip, squatting on the carpet at his feet, staring into the coals; and Polynesia perched on the mantelpiece beside his shabby high hat, gravely swinging her head from side to side in time to the music. I see it all, just as though it were before me now.

And then I remember how, after we had seen the Doctor out at the front door, we all came back into the parlour and talked about him till it was still later, and even after I did go to bed (I had never stayed up so late in my life before) I dreamed about him and a band of strange, clever animals that played flutes and fiddles and drums the whole night through.

Chapter Seven
SHELLFISH TALK

THE next morning, although I had gone to bed so late the night before, I was up frightfully early. The first sparrows were just beginning to chirp sleepily on the slates outside my attic window when I jumped out of bed and scrambled into my clothes.

I could hardly wait to get back to the little house with the big garden – to see the Doctor and his private zoo. For the first time in my life I forgot all about breakfast; and creeping down the stairs on tiptoe, so as not to wake my mother and father, I opened the front door and popped out into the empty, silent street.

When I got to the Doctor's gate I suddenly thought that perhaps it was too early to call on anyone, and I began to wonder if the

Doctor would be up yet. I looked into the garden. No one seemed to be about. So I opened the gate quietly and went inside.

As I turned to the left to go down a path between some hedges, I heard a voice quite close to me say, 'Good morning. How early you are!'

I turned around, and there, sitting on the top of a privet hedge, was the grey parrot, Polynesia.

'Good morning,' I said. 'I suppose I am rather early. Is the Doctor still in bed?'

'Oh, no,' said Polynesia. 'He has been up an hour and a half. You'll find him in the house somewhere. The front door is open. Just push it and go in. He is sure to be in the kitchen cooking breakfast – or working in his study. Walk right in. I am waiting to see the sun rise. But, upon my word, I believe it's forgotten to rise. It is an awful climate, this. Now if we were in Africa the world would be blazing with sunlight at this hour of the morning. Just see that mist rolling over those cabbages. It is enough to give you rheumatism to look at it . Beastly climate – beastly! Really, I don't know why anything but frogs ever stay in England. Well, don't let me keep you. Run along and see the Doctor.'

'Thank you,' I said. 'I'll go and look for him.'

When I opened the front door I could smell bacon frying, so I made my way to the kitchen. There I discovered a large kettle boiling away over the fire and some bacon and eggs in a dish upon the hearth. It seemed to me that the bacon was getting all dried up with the heat. So I pulled the dish a little farther away from the fire and went on through the house looking for the Doctor.

I found him at last in the study. I did not know then that it was called the study. It was certainly a very interesting room, with telescopes and microscopes and all sorts of other strange things that I did not understand but wished I did. Hanging on the walls were pictures of animals and fishes and strange plants and collections of birds' eggs and seashells in glass cases.

The Doctor was standing at the main table in his dressing gown. At first I thought he was washing his face. He had a square glass box before him full of water. He was holding one ear under the water, while he covered the other with his left hand. As I came in he stood up.

'Good morning, Stubbins,' said he. 'Going

to be a nice day, don't you think? I've just been listening to the Wiff-Waff. But he is very disappointing – very.'

'Why?' I said. 'Didn't you find that he has any language at all?'

'Oh, yes,' said the Doctor, 'he has a language. But it is such a poor language – only a few words, like "yes" and "no", "hot" and "cold". That's all he can say. It's very disappointing. You see, he really belongs to two different families of fishes. I thought he was going to be tremendously helpful . . . well, well!'

'I suppose,' said I, 'that means he hasn't very much sense – if his language is only two or three words?'

'Yes, I suppose it does. Possibly it is the kind of life he leads. You see, they are very rare now, these Wiff-Waffs, very rare and very solitary. They swim around in the deepest parts of the ocean entirely by themselves – always alone. So I presume they really don't need to talk much.'

'Perhaps some kind of a bigger shellfish would talk more,' I said. 'After all, he is very small, isn't he?'

'Yes,' said the Doctor, 'that's true. Oh, I have no doubt that there are shellfish who are good talkers — not the least doubt. But the big shellfish — the biggest of them are so hard to catch. They are to be found only in the deep parts of the sea; and as they don't swim very much, but just crawl along the floor of the ocean most of the time, they are very seldom taken in nets. I do wish I could find some way of going down to the bottom of the sea. I could learn a lot if I could only do that. But we are forgetting all about breakfast. . . . Have you had breakfast yet, Stubbins?'

I told the Doctor that I had forgotten all about it and he at once led the way into the kitchen.

'Yes,' he said, as he poured the hot water from the kettle into the teapot, 'if a man could only manage to get right down to the bottom of the sea and live there a while, he would discover some wonderful things — things that people have never dreamed of.'

'But men do go down, don't they?' I asked, '. . . divers and people like that?'

'Oh, yes, to be sure,' said the Doctor. 'Divers go down. I've been down myself in a diving suit, for that matter. But, my! — They go only where the sea is shallow. Divers can't go down where it is really deep.

What I would like to do is to go down to the great depths – where it is miles deep. Well, well, I dare say I shall manage it some day. Let me give you another cup of tea.'

Chapter Eight
ARE YOU A GOOD NOTICER?

JUST at that moment Polynesia came into the room and said something to the Doctor in bird language. Of course I did not understand what it was. But the Doctor at once put down his knife and fork and left the room.

'You know, it is an awful shame,' said the parrot as soon as the Doctor had closed the door. 'Directly he comes back home, all the animals over the whole countryside get to hear of it and every sick cat and mangy rabbit for miles around comes to see him and ask his advice. Now there's a big fat hare outside at the back door with a squawking baby. Can she see the Doctor, please! Thinks it's going to have convulsions. Stupid little thing's been eating deadly nightshade again, I suppose. The animals are *so* inconsiderate at times — especially the mothers. They come round and call the Doctor away from his meals and wake him out of his bed at all hours of the night. I don't know how he stands it — really, I don't. Why, the poor man never gets any peace at all! I've told him time and again to have special hours for the animals to come. But he is so frightfully kind and considerate. He never refuses to see them if there is anything really wrong with them. He says the urgent cases must be seen at once.'

'Why don't some of the animals go and see the other doctors?' I asked.

'Oh, good gracious!' exclaimed the parrot, tossing her head scornfully. 'Why, there aren't any other animal doctors — not real doctors. Oh, of course there *are* those vet persons, to be sure. But, bless you, they're no good. You see, they can't understand the animals' language, so how can you expect them to be any use? Imagine yourself, or your father, going to see a doctor who could not understand a word you say — nor even tell you in your own language what you must do to get well! Poof! — those vets!

They're that stupid, you've no idea! Put the Doctor's bacon down by the fire, will you, to keep hot till he comes back.'

'Do you think I would ever be able to learn the language of the animals?' I asked, laying the plate upon the hearth.

'Well, it all depends,' said Polynesia. 'Are you clever at lessons?'

'I don't know,' I answered, feeling rather ashamed. 'You see, I've never been to school. My father is too poor to send me.'

'Well,' said the parrot, 'I don't suppose you have really missed much – to judge from what *I* have seen of schoolboys. But listen: Are you a good noticer? Do you notice things well? I mean, for instance, supposing you saw two cock starlings on an apple tree, and you took only one good look at them – would you be able to tell one from the other if you saw them again the next day?'

'I don't know,' I said. 'I've never tried.'

'Well, that . . .' said Polynesia, brushing some crumbs off the corner of the table with her left foot, 'that is what you call powers of observation – noticing the small things about birds and animals: the way they walk and move their heads and flip their wings; the way they sniff the air and twitch their whiskers and wiggle their tails. You have to notice all those little things if you want to learn animal language. For, you see, lots of the animals hardly talk at all with their tongues; they use their breath or their tails or their feet, instead. That is because many of them, in the olden days when lions and tigers were more plentiful, were afraid to make a noise for fear the savage creatures would hear them. Birds, of course, didn't care, for they always had wings to fly away with. But that is the first thing to remember: being a good noticer is terribly important in learning animal language.'

'It sounds pretty hard,' I said.

'You'll have to be very patient,' said Polynesia. 'It takes a long time to say even a few words properly. But if you come here often, I'll give you a few lessons myself. And once you get started, you'll be surprised how fast you get on. It would indeed be a good thing if you could learn. Because then you could do some of the work for the Doctor – I mean the easier work, like bandaging and giving pills. Yes, yes, that's a good idea of mine. 'Twould be a great thing if the poor man could get some help – and some rest. It is a scandal the way he works. I see no reason

' "Being a good noticer is terribly important" '

why you shouldn't be able to help him a great deal — that is, if you are really interested in animals.'

'Oh, I'd love that!' I cried. 'Do you think the Doctor would let me?'

'Certainly,' said Polynesia, 'as soon as you have learned something about doctoring. I'll speak of it to him myself — sh! I hear him coming. Quick — bring his bacon back to the table.'

Chapter Nine
THE GARDEN OF DREAMS

WHEN breakfast was over the Doctor took me out to show me the garden. Well, if the house had been interesting, the garden was a hundred times more so. At first, you did not realize how big it was. When you were sure that you had seen it all, you would peer over a hedge or turn a corner and look up some steps, and there was a whole new part.

It had everything. There were wide lawns with carved stone seats, green with moss. Over the lawns hung weeping willows, and their feathery bough tips brushed the velvet grass when they swung with the wind. The old flagged paths had high clipped yew hedges on either side of them, so that they looked like the narrow streets of some old town; and through the hedges, doorways had been made; and over the doorways were shapes like vases and peacocks and half-moons all trimmed out of the living trees. There was a lovely marble fishpond with golden carp and blue water lilies in it and big green frogs. A high brick wall alongside the kitchen garden was all covered with pink and yellow peaches ripening in the sun. There was a wonderful great oak, hollow in the trunk, big enough for four men to hide inside. Many summer-houses there were, too — some of wood and some of stone — and one of them was full of books to read. In a corner, among some rocks and ferns, was an outdoor fire-place, where the Doctor used to fry liver and bacon when he had a notion to take his meals in the open air. There was a couch as well on which he used to sleep, it seems, on warm summer nights when the nightingales were singing at their best; it had wheels on it so it could be moved about under any tree they sang in. But the thing that fascinated me most of all was a tiny little tree house high up in the top branches of a great elm, with a long rope ladder leading to it. The Doctor told me he used it for looking at the moon and the stars through a telescope.

It was the kind of a garden where you could wander and explore for days and days – always coming upon something new, always glad to find the old spots over again. That first time that I saw the Doctor's garden I was so charmed by it that I felt I would like to live in it and never go outside of it again. For it had everything within its walls to make living pleasant – to keep the heart at peace. It was the garden of dreams.

There were a lot of birds about. Every tree seemed to have two or three nests in it. And heaps of other wild creatures appeared to be making themselves at home there, too. Stoats and tortoises and dormice seemed to be quite common, and not in the least shy. Toads of different colours and sizes hopped about the lawn as though it belonged to them. Green lizards (which were very rare in Puddleby) sat up on the stones in the sunlight and blinked at us. Even snakes were to be seen.

'You need not be afraid of them,' said the Doctor, noticing that I started somewhat when a large black snake wiggled across the path right in front of us. 'These fellows are not poisonous. They do a great deal of good in keeping down many kinds of garden pests. I play the flute to them sometimes in the evening. They love it. Stand right up on their tails and carry on no end. Funny thing, their taste for music.'

'Why do all these animals come and live here?' I asked. 'I never saw a garden with so many creatures in it.'

'Well, I suppose it's because they get the kind of food they like, and nobody worries or disturbs them. And then, of course, they know me. And if they or their children get sick, I presume they find it handy to be living in a doctor's garden. Look! You see that sparrow on the sundial, swearing at the blackbird down below? Well, he has been coming here every summer for years. He comes from London. The country sparrows round about here are always laughing at him. They say he chirps with such a cockney accent. He is a most amusing bird – very brave but very cheeky. He loves nothing better than an argument, but he always ends it by getting rude. He is a real city bird. In London he lives around St. Paul's Cathedral. "Cheapside", we call him.'

'Are all these birds from the country round here?' I asked.

'Most of them,' said the Doctor. 'But a few

rare ones visit me every year who ordinarily never come near England at all. For instance, that handsome little fellow hovering over the snapdragon there, he's a ruby-throated hummingbird. Comes from America. Strictly speaking, he has no business in this climate at all. It is too cool. I make him sleep in the kitchen at night. Then every August, about the last week of the month, I have a purple bird of paradise come all the way from Brazil to see me. She is a very great swell. Hasn't arrived yet, of course. And there are a few others, foreign birds from the tropics, mostly, who drop in on me in the course of the summer months. But come, I must show you the zoo.'

Chapter Ten
THE PRIVATE ZOO

I DID not think there could be anything left in that garden that we had not seen. But the Doctor took me by the arm and we soon found ourselves before a small door in a high stone wall. The Doctor pushed it open.

Inside was still another garden. I had expected to find cages with animals inside them. But there were none to be seen. Instead there were little stone houses all over the garden, and each house had a window and a door. As we walked in, many of these doors opened and animals came running out to us, evidently expecting food.

'Haven't the doors any locks on them?' I asked the Doctor.

'Oh, yes,' he said, 'every door has a lock. But in my zoo the doors open from the inside, not from the out. The locks are there only so the animals can go and shut themselves *in* any time they want to get away from the annoyance of other animals or from people who might come here. Every animal in this zoo stays here because he likes it, not because he is made to.'

'They all look very happy and clean,' I said. 'Would you mind telling me the names of some of them?'

'Certainly. Well, now, that funny-looking thing with plates on his back, nosing under the brick over there, is a South American armadillo. The little chap talking to him is a Canadian woodchuck. They both live in those holes you see at the foot of the wall. The two little beasts doing antics in the pond are a pair of Russian minks. . . . And that reminds me, I must go and get them some herrings from the town before noon — it is early closing today. That animal just stepping out of his house is an antelope, one of the smaller South African kinds. Now let us move to the other side of those bushes there and I will show you some more.'

'Are those deer over there?' I asked.

'*Deer!*' said the Doctor. 'Where do you mean?'

'Over there,' I said, pointing, 'nibbling the grass border of the bed. There are two of them.'

'Oh, that,' said the Doctor with a smile. 'That isn't two animals: that's one animal with two heads — the only two-headed animal in the world. It's called the pushmi-pullyu. I brought him from Africa. He's very tame — acts as a kind of night watchman for my zoo. He sleeps with only one head at a time, you see — very handy. The other head stays awake all night.'

'Have you any lions or tigers?' I asked as we moved on.

'No,' said the Doctor. 'It wouldn't be possible to keep them here — and I wouldn't keep them even if I could. If I had my way, Stubbins, there wouldn't be a single lion or tiger in captivity anywhere in the world. They're never happy. They never settle down. They are always thinking of the big countries they have left behind. You can see it in their eyes, dreaming always of the great open spaces; dreaming of the dark jungles where their mothers first taught them how to scent and track the deer. And what are they given in exchange for all this?' asked the Doctor, stopping in his walk and growing all red and angry. For the glory of an African sunrise, for the twilight breeze whispering through the palms, for the green shade of the matted, tangled vines, for the cool, big-starred nights of the desert, for the patter of the waterfall after a hard day's hunt? Why, a bare cage with iron bars, an ugly piece of dead meat thrust in to them once a day, and a crowd of fools to come and stare at them with open mouths! No, Stubbins, lions and tigers, the big hunters, should never, never be seen in zoos.'

The Doctor seemed to have grown terribly serious – almost sad. But suddenly his manner changed again and he took me by the arm with his same old cheerful smile.

'But we haven't seen the butterfly houses yet – nor the aquariums. Come along. I am very proud of my butterfly houses.'

Off we went again and came presently into a hedged enclosure. Here I saw several big huts made of fine wire netting, like cages. Inside the netting all sorts of beautiful flowers were growing in the sun, with butter-flies skimming over them. The Doctor pointed to the end of one of the huts, where little boxes with holes in them stood in a row.

'Those are the hatching boxes,' said he.

'There I put different kinds of caterpillars. And as soon as they turn into butterflies and moths, they come out into these flower-gardens to feed.'

'Do butterflies have a language?' I asked.

'Oh, I fancy they have,' said the Doctor, 'and the beetles, too. But so far I haven't succeeded in learning much about insect languages. I have been too busy lately trying to master the shellfish talk. I mean to take it up, though.'

At that moment Polynesia joined us and said, 'Doctor, there are two guinea pigs at the back door. They say they have run away from the boy who kept them because they didn't get the right stuff to eat. They want to know if you will take them in.'

'All right,' said the Doctor. 'Show them the way to the zoo. Give them the house on the left, near the gate – the one the black fox had. Tell them what the rules are and give them a square meal. Now, Stubbins, we will go on to the aquarium. And first of all I must show you my big glass sea-water tank, where I keep the shellfish.'

Chapter Eleven
MY SCHOOLTEACHER,
POLYNESIA

WELL, there were not many days
after that, when I did not come to see my
new friend. Indeed I was at his house practically all day and every day. So that one
evening my mother asked me jokingly why
I did not take my bed over there and live at
the Doctor's house altogether.

After a while I think I got to be quite
useful to the Doctor, feeding his pets for
him; helping to make new houses and fences
for the zoo; assisting with the sick animals
that came; doing odd jobs about the place. So
that although I enjoyed it all very much, I
really think the Doctor would have missed
me if I had not come so often.

And all this time Polynesia came with me
wherever I went, teaching me bird language

and showing me how to understand the talking signs of the animals. At first I thought I would never be able to learn at all — it seemed so difficult. But the old parrot was wonderfully patient with me — though I could see that occasionally she had hard work to keep her temper.

Soon I began to pick up the strange chatter of the birds and to understand the funny talking antics of the dogs. I used to practise listening to the mice behind the wainscot after I went to bed.

And the days passed very quickly and turned into weeks, and weeks into months, and soon the roses in the Doctor's garden were losing their petals and yellow leaves lay upon the wide green lawn. For the summer was nearly gone.

One day Polynesia and I were talking in the library. Polynesia was showing me the books about animals that John Dolittle had written himself.

'My!' I said. 'What a lot of books the Doctor has — all the way around the room! Goodness! I wish I could read! It must be tremendously interesting. Can you read, Polynesia?'

'Only a little,' said she. 'Be careful how

you turn those pages – don't tear them. No, I really don't get time enough for reading much. That letter there is a *k* and this is a *b*.'

'What does this word under the picture mean?' I asked.

'Let me see,' she said and started spelling it out. 'B-A-B-O-O-N – that's *monkey*. Reading isn't nearly as hard as it looks, once you know the letters.'

'Polynesia,' I said, 'I want to ask you something very important.'

'What is it, my boy?' said she, smoothing down the feathers of her right wing. Polynesia often spoke to me in a very patronizing way. But I did not mind it from her. After all, she was nearly two hundred years old, and I was only ten.

'Listen,' I said, 'my mother doesn't think it is right that I come here for so many meals. And I was going to ask you: supposing I did a whole lot more work for the Doctor – why couldn't I come and live here, altogether? You see, instead of being paid like a regular gardener or workman, I would get my bed and meals in exchange for the work I did. What do you think?'

'You mean you want to be a proper assistant to the Doctor, is that it?'

'Yes. I suppose that's what you call it,' I answered. 'You know you said yourself that you thought I could be very useful to him.'

'Well' – she thought a moment – 'I really don't see why not. But is this what you want to be when you grow up, a naturalist?'

'Yes,' I said, 'I have made up my mind. I would sooner be a naturalist than anything else in the world.'

'Humph! Let's go and speak to the Doctor about it,' said Polynesia. 'He's in the next room – in the study. Open the door very gently – he may be working and not want to be disturbed.'

I opened the door quietly and peeped in. The first thing I saw was an enormous black retriever dog sitting in the middle of the hearthrug with his ears cocked up, listening to the Doctor who was reading aloud to him from a letter.

'What *is* the Doctor doing?' I asked Polynesia in a whisper.

'Oh, the dog has had a letter from his mistress and he has brought it to the Doctor to read for him, that's all. He belongs to a funny little girl called Minnie Dooley, who lives on the other side of the town. She has pigtails down her back. She and her brother have gone away to the seaside for the summer, and the old retriever is heart-broken while the children are gone. So they write letters to him – in English, of course. And as the old dog doesn't understand them, he brings them here and the Doctor turns them into dog language for him. I think Minnie must have written that she is coming back – to judge from the dog's excitement. Just look at him carrying on!'

Indeed the retriever seemed to be suddenly overcome with joy. As the Doctor finished the letter the old dog started barking at the top of his voice, wagging his tail wildly and jumping about the study. He took the letter in his mouth and ran out of the room snorting hard and mumbling to himself.

'He's going down to meet the coach,' whispered Polynesia. 'That dog's devotion to those children is more than I can understand. You should see Minnie! She's the most conceited little minx that ever walked. She squints, too.'

Chapter Twelve
MY GREAT IDEA

PRESENTLY the Doctor looked up and saw us at the door.

'Oh, come in, Stubbins,' said he. 'Did you wish to speak to me? Come in and take a chair.'

'Doctor,' I said, 'I want to be a naturalist — like you — when I grow up.'

'Oh you do, do you?' murmured the Doctor. 'Humph! . . . Well! . . . Dear me! . . . You don't say! . . . well, well! Have you, er, have you spoken to your mother and father about it?'

'No, not yet,' I said. 'I want you to speak to them for me. You would do it better. I want to be your helper — your assistant, if you'll have me. Last night my mother was saying that she didn't consider it right for me to come here so often for meals. And I've been thinking about it a good deal since. Couldn't we make some arrangement – couldn't I work for my meals and sleep here?'

'But my dear Stubbins,' said the Doctor, laughing, 'you are quite welcome to come here for three meals a day all year round. I'm only too glad to have you. Besides, you do do a lot of work, as it is. I've often felt that I ought to pay you for what you do. . . . But what arrangement was it that you thought of?'

'Well, I thought,' said I, 'that perhaps you would come and see my mother and father and tell them that if they let me live here with you and work hard, that you will teach me to read and write. You see, my mother is awfully anxious to have me learn reading and writing. And besides, I couldn't be a proper naturalist without, could I?'

'Oh, I don't know so much about that,' said the Doctor. 'It is nice, I admit, to be able to read and write. But the greatest naturalist of them all doesn't even know how to write his own name or to read the ABC.'

'Who is he?' I asked.

'He is a mysterious person,' said the Doctor, '– a very mysterious person. His name is Long Arrow, the son of Golden Arrow. He is an Indian.'

'Have you ever seen him?' I asked.

'No,' said the Doctor, 'I've never seen him. No European has ever met him. He lives almost entirely with animals and with the different tribes of Indians – usually somewhere among the mountains of Peru. Never stays long in one place. Goes from tribe to tribe, like a sort of tramp.'

'How do you know so much about him,' I asked, 'if you've never even seen him?'

'The purple bird of paradise,' said the Doctor, 'she told me all about him. She says he is a perfectly marvellous naturalist. I got her to take a message to him from me last time she was here. I am expecting her back any day now. I can hardly wait to see what answer she has brought from him. It is already almost the last week of August. I do hope nothing has happened to her on the way.'

'But why do the animals and birds come to you when they are sick?' I said. 'Why don't they go to him, if he is so very wonderful?'

'It seems that my methods are more up-to-date,' said the Doctor. 'But from what the purple bird of paradise tells me, Long

Arrow's knowledge of natural history must be positively tremendous. His speciality is botany – plants and all that sort of thing. But he knows a lot about birds and animals, too. He's very good on bees and beetles. . . . But now, tell me, Stubbins, are you quite sure that you really want to be a naturalist?'

'Yes,' said I, 'my mind is made up.'

'Well, you know, it isn't a very good profession for making money. Most of the good naturalists don't make any money whatever. All they do is *spend* money, buying butterfly nets and cases for birds' eggs and things. It is only now, after I have been a naturalist for many years, that I am beginning to make a little money from the books I write.'

'I don't care about money,' I said. 'I want to be a naturalist. Won't you please come and have dinner with my mother and father next Thursday? I told them I was going to ask you – and then you can talk to them about it. You see, there's another thing: if I'm living with you and sort of belong to your house and business, I shall be able to come with you next time you go on a voyage.'

'Oh, I see,' said he, smiling. 'So you want to come on a voyage with me, do you? Aha!'

'I want to go on all your voyages with you. It would be much easier for you if you had someone to carry the butterfly nets and notebooks, wouldn't it now?'

For a long time the Doctor sat thinking, drumming on the desk with his fingers while I waited, terribly impatiently, to see what he was going to say.

At last he shrugged his shoulders and stood up.

'Well, Stubbins,' said he, 'I'll come and talk it over with you and your parents next Thursday. And – well, we'll see. We'll see. Give your mother and father my compliments and thank them for their invitation, will you?'

Then I tore home like the wind to tell my mother that the Doctor had promised to come.

Chapter Thirteen
A TRAVELLER ARRIVES

THE next day I was sitting on the wall of the Doctor's garden after tea, talking to Dab-Dab. I had now learned so much from Polynesia that I could talk to most birds and some animals without a great deal of difficulty. I found Dab-Dab a very nice old motherly bird – though not nearly so clever and interesting as Polynesia. She had been housekeeper for the Doctor many years now.

Well, as I was saying, the old duck and I were sitting on the flat top of the garden wall that evening, looking down on the Oxenthorpe Road below. We were watching some sheep being driven to market in Puddleby, and Dab-Dab had just been telling me about the Doctor's adventures in

'A traveller arrives'

Africa. For she had gone on a voyage there
with him long ago.

Suddenly I heard a curious distant noise
down the road towards the town. It sounded
like a lot of people cheering. I stood up on
the wall to see if I could make out what was
coming. Presently there appeared round a
bend a great crowd of schoolchildren following a very ragged, curious-looking woman.

'What in the world can it be?' cried
Dab-Dab.

The children were all laughing and
shouting. And certainly the woman they
were following was most extraordinary. She
had very long arms and the most stooping
shoulders I have ever seen. She wore a straw
hat on the side of her head with poppies on
it, and her skirt was so long for her it
dragged on the ground like a ball gown's
train. I could not see anything of her face
because of the wide hat pulled over her eyes.
But as she got nearer to us and the laughing
of the children grew louder, I noticed that
her hands were very dark in colour and
hairy, like a witch's.

Then all of a sudden Dab-Dab at my side
startled me by crying out in a loud voice,
'Why, it's Chee-Chee! Chee-Chee come back

at last! How dare those children tease him!
I'll give the little imps something to laugh
at!'

And she flew right off the wall down to the
street and made straight for the children,
squawking away in a most terrifying
fashion and pecking at their feet and legs.
The children made off down the street back
to the town as hard as they could run.

The strange-looking figure in the straw
hat stood gazing after them a moment and
then came wearily up to the gate. It didn't
bother to undo the latch but just climbed
right over the gate as though it were
something in the way. And then I noticed
that it took hold of the bars with its feet, so
that it really had four hands to climb with.
But it was only when I at last got a glimpse
of the face under the hat that I could be
really sure it was a monkey.

Chee-Chee – for it was he – frowned at
me suspiciously from the top of the gate, as
though he thought I was going to laugh at
him like the other boys and girls. Then he
dropped into the garden on the inside and
immediately started taking off his clothes.
He tore the straw hat in two and threw it
down into the street. Then he took off his

bodice and skirt, jumped on them savagely, and began kicking them round the front garden.

Presently I heard a screech from the house, and out flew Polynesia, followed by the Doctor and Jip.

'Chee-Chee! Chee-Chee!' shouted the parrot. 'You've come at last! I always told the Doctor you'd find a way. How ever did you do it?'

They all gathered round him, shaking him by his four hands, laughing and asking him a million questions at once. Then they all started back for the house.

'Run up to my bedroom, Stubbins,' said the Doctor, turning to me. 'You'll find a bag of peanuts in the small left-hand drawer of the bureau. I have always kept them there in case he might come back unexpectedly some day. And wait a minute – see if Dab-Dab has any bananas in the pantry. Chee-Chee hasn't had a banana, he tells me, in two months.'

When I came down again to the kitchen I found everybody listening attentively to the monkey, who was telling the story of his journey from Africa.

Chapter Fourteen
CHEE-CHEE'S VOYAGE

IT seems that after Polynesia had left, Chee-Chee had grown more homesick than ever for the Doctor and the little house in Puddleby. At last he had made up his mind that by hook or crook he would follow her. And one day, going down to the seashore, he saw a lot of people getting on to a ship that was coming to England. He tried to get on too. But they turned him back and drove him away. And presently he noticed a whole big family of people passing on to the ship. And one of the children in this family reminded Chee-Chee of a cousin of his with whom he had once been in love. So he said to himself, 'That girl looks just as much like a monkey as I look like a girl. If I could only get some clothes to wear I might easily slip on to the ship among these families, and people would take me for a girl. Good idea!'

So he went off to a house that was quite close, and hopping in through a open window he found a skirt and bodice lying on a chair. They belonged to a fashionable lady who was taking a bath. Chee-Chee put them on. Next he went back to the seashore, mingled with the crowd there, and at last sneaked safely on to the big ship. Then he thought he had better hide, for fear people might look at him too closely. And he stayed hidden all the time the ship was sailing to England – only coming out at night, when everybody was asleep, to find food.

When he reached England and tried to get off the ship, the sailors saw at last that he was only a monkey dressed up in girl's clothes, and they wanted to keep him for a pet. But he managed to give them the slip; and once he was on shore, he dived into the crowd and got away. But he was still a long distance from Puddleby and had to come right across the whole breadth of England.

He had a terrible time of it. Whenever he passed through a town all the children caught hold of him and tried to stop him, so that he had to run up lamp-posts and climb

to chimney pots to escape from them. At
night he used to sleep in ditches or barns or
anywhere he could hide, and he lived on the
berries he picked from the hedges and the
cobnuts that grew in the copses. At length,
after many adventures and narrow squeaks,
he saw the tower of Puddleby Church and he
knew that at last he was near his old home.

When Chee-Chee had finished his story he
ate six bananas without stopping and drank
a whole bowlful of milk.

'My!' he said. 'Why wasn't I born with
wings, like Polynesia, so I could fly here?
You've no idea how I grew to hate that hat
and skirt. I've never been so uncomfortable
in my life. All the way from Bristol here, if
the wretched hat wasn't falling off my head
or catching in the trees, those beastly skirts
were tripping me up and getting wound
round everything. What on earth do women
wear those things for? Goodness, I was glad
to see old Puddleby this morning when I
climbed over the hill by Bellaby's farm!'

'Your bed on top of the plate rack in the
scullery is all ready for you,' said the Doctor.
'We never had it disturbed, in case you
might come back.'

'Yes,' said Dab-Dab, 'and you can have the

old smoking jacket of the Doctor's, which you used to use as a blanket, in case it is cold in the night.'

'Thanks,' said Chee-Chee. 'It's good to be back in the old house again. Everything's just the same as when I left, except the clean roller towel on the back of the door there — that's new. Well, I think I'll go to bed now. I need sleep.'

Then we all went out of the kitchen into the scullery and watched Chee-Chee climb the plate rack like a sailor going up a mast. On the top, he curled himself up, pulled the old smoking jacket over him, and in a minute he was snoring peacefully.

'Good old Chee-Chee!' whispered the Doctor. 'I'm glad he's back.'

'Yes, good old Chee-Chee!' echoed Dab-Dab and Polynesia.

Then we all tiptoed out of the scullery and closed the door very gently behind us.

Chapter Fifteen
I BECOME A DOCTOR'S ASSISTANT

WHEN Thursday evening came, there was great excitement at our house. My mother had asked me what were the Doctor's favourite dishes, and I had told her: spare ribs, sliced beetroot, fried bread, shrimps and treacle tart. Tonight she had them all on the table waiting for him and she was fussing round the house to see if everything was tidy and in readiness for his coming.

At last we heard a knock upon the door, and of course it was I who got there first to let him in.

The Doctor had brought his own flute with him this time. And after supper was over, the table was cleared away and the Doctor and my father started playing duets.

They got so interested in this that I began to be afraid that they would never come to talking over my business. But at last the Doctor said, 'Your son tells me that he is anxious to become a naturalist.'

And then began a long talk, which lasted far into the night. At first both my mother and father were rather against the idea – as they had been from the beginning. They said it was only a boyish whim, and that I would get tired of it very soon.

But after the matter had been talked over from every side, the Doctor turned to my father and said, 'Well, now, supposing, Mr Stubbins, that your son came to me for two years – that is, until he is twelve years old. During those two years he will have time to see if he is going to grow tired of it or not. Also, during that time, I will promise to teach him reading and writing and perhaps a little arithmetic as well. What do you say to that?'

'I don't know,' said my father, shaking his head. 'You are very kind and it is a handsome offer you make, Doctor. But I feel that Tommy ought to be learning some trade by which he can earn his living later on.'

Then my mother spoke up. Although she

was nearly in tears at the prospect of my leaving her house while I was so young, she pointed out to my father that this was a grand chance for me to get learning.

'Now, Jacob,' she said, 'you know that many lads in the town have been to the grammar school till they were fourteen or fifteen years old. Tommy can easily spare these two years for his education; and if he learns no more than to read and write, the time will not be lost. Though goodness knows,' she added, getting out her handkerchief to cry, 'the house will seem terribly empty when he's gone.'

'I will take care that he comes to see you, Mrs Stubbins,' said the Doctor, 'every day, if you like. After all, he will not be very far away.'

Well, at length my father gave in, and it was agreed that I was to live with the Doctor and work for him for two years in exchange for learning to read and write and for my board and lodging.

'Of course,' added the Doctor, 'while I have money I will keep Tommy in clothes as well. But money is a very irregular thing with me; sometimes I have some, and then sometimes I haven't.'

'You are very good, Doctor,' said my mother, drying her tears. 'It seems to me that Tommy is a very fortunate boy.'

And then, thoughtless, selfish little imp that I was, I leaned over and whispered in the Doctor's ear, 'Please don't forget to say something about the voyages.'

'Oh, by the way,' said John Dolittle, 'of course occasionally my work requires me to travel. You will have no objection, I take it, to your son's coming with me?'

My poor mother looked up sharply, more unhappy and anxious than ever at this new turn, while I stood behind the Doctor's chair, my heart thumping with excitement, waiting for my father's answer.

'No,' he said slowly after a while. 'If we agree to the other arrangement, I don't see that we've the right to make any objection to that.'

Well, there surely was never a happier boy in the world than I was at that moment. At last the dream of my life was to come true! For I knew perfectly well that it was now almost time for the Doctor to start upon another voyage. Polynesia had told me that he hardly ever stayed at home for more than six months at a stretch. Therefore he would

be surely going again within a fortnight.
And I – I, Tommy Stubbins, would go with
him! Just to think of it! – To cross the sea,
to walk on foreign shores, to roam the
world!

PART II

Chapter One
THE CREW OF *THE CURLEW*

FROM that time on, of course, my position in the town was very different. I was no longer a poor cobbler's son. I carried my nose in the air as I went down the High Street with Jip in his gold collar at my side; and snobbish little boys who had despised me before because I was not rich enough to go to school now pointed me out to their friends and whispered, 'You see him? He's a doctor's assistant – and only ten years old!'

Two days after the Doctor had been to our house to dinner he told me very sadly that he was afraid that he would have to give up trying to learn the language of the shell-fish – in any event, for the present.

'I'm very discouraged, Stubbins, very. I've tried the mussels and the clams, the oysters and the whelks, cockles and scallops, seven different kinds of crabs, and all the lobster family. I think I'll leave it for the present and go at it again later on.'

'What will you turn to now?' I asked.

'Well, I rather thought of going on a voyage, Stubbins. It's quite a time now since I've been away. And there is great deal of work waiting for me abroad.'

'When shall we start?' I asked.

'Well, first I shall have to wait till the purple bird of paradise gets here. I must see if she has any message for me from Long Arrow. She's late. She should have been here ten days ago. I hope to goodness she's all right.'

'Well, hadn't we better be seeing about getting a boat?' I said. 'She is sure to be here in a day or so, and there will be lots of things to do to get ready in the meantime, won't there?'

'Yes, indeed,' said the Doctor. 'Suppose we go down and see your friend Joe, the mussel man. He will know about boats.'

'I'd like to come too,' said Jip.

'All right, come along,' said the Doctor, and off we went.

Joe said, yes he had a boat — one he had

just bought — but it needed three people to sail her. We told him we would like to see it anyway.

So the mussel man took us off a little way down the river and showed us the neatest, prettiest little vessel that ever was built. She was called *The Curlew*. Joe said he would sell her to us cheap. But the trouble was that the boat needed three people, while we were only two.

'Of course I shall be taking Chee-Chee,' said the Doctor. 'But although he is very quick and clever, he is not as strong as a man. We really ought to have another person to sail a boat as big as that.'

'I know of a good sailor, Doctor,' said Joe, 'a first-class seaman who would be glad of the job.'

'No, thank you, Joe,' said Doctor Dolittle. 'I don't want any seamen. I couldn't afford to hire them. And then they hamper me so, seamen do, when I'm at sea. They're always wanting to do things the proper way, and I like to do them *my* way. Now let me see: who could we take with us?'

'There's Matthew Mugg, the cat's-meat man,' I said.

'No, he wouldn't do. Matthew's a very nice

fellow, but he talks too much – mostly about his rheumatism. You have to be frightfully particular whom you take with you on long voyages.'

'How about Luke the Hermit?' I asked.

'That's a good idea – splendid – if he'll come. Let's go and ask him right away.'

Chapter Two
LUKE THE HERMIT

THE Hermit was an old friend of ours. He was a very peculiar person. Far out on the marshes he lived in a little bit of a shack — all alone except for his brindle bulldog. He never came into the town, never seemed to want to see or talk to people. His dog, Bob, drove them away if they came near his hut. When you asked anyone in Puddleby who he was or why he lived out in that lonely place by himself, the only answer you got was 'Oh, Luke the Hermit? Well, there's some mystery about him. Nobody knows what it is. But there's a mystery. Don't go near him. He'll set the dog on you.'

Nevertheless there were two people who often went out to the little shack on the fens:

the Doctor and myself. And Bob, the bulldog, never barked when he heard us coming. For we liked Luke, and Luke liked us.

This afternoon, crossing the marshes we faced a cold wind blowing from the east. As we approached the hut Jip put up his ears and said, 'That's funny!'

'What's funny?' asked the Doctor.

'That Bob hasn't come out to meet us. He should have heard us long ago — or smelled us. What's that queer noise?'

'Sounds to me like a gate creaking,' said the Doctor. 'Maybe it's Luke's door, only we can't see the door from here; it's on the far side of the shack.'

'I hope Bob isn't sick,' said Jip, and he let out a bark to see if that would call him. But the only answer he got was the wailing of the wind across the wide salt fen.

We hurried forward, all three of us thinking hard.

When we reached the front of the shack we found the door open, swinging and creaking dismally in the wind. We looked inside. There was no one there.

'Isn't Luke at home, then?' said I. 'Perhaps he's out for a walk.'

'He is *always* at home,' said the Doctor, frowning in a peculiar sort of way. 'And even if he were out for a walk, he wouldn't leave his door banging in the wind behind him. There is something queer about this. . . . What are you doing in there Jip?'

'Nothing much – nothing worth speaking of,' said Jip, examining the floor of the hut extremely carefully.

'Come here, Jip,' said the Doctor in a stern voice. 'You are hiding something from me. You see signs and you know something – or you guess it. What has happened? Tell me. Where is the Hermit?'

'I don't know,' said Jip, looking very guilty and uncomfortable. 'I don't know where he is.'

'Well, you know something. I can tell it from the look in your eye. What is it?'

But Jip didn't answer.

For ten minutes the Doctor kept questioning him. But not a word would the dog say.

'Well,' said the Doctor at last, 'it is no use our standing around here in the cold. The Hermit's gone. That's all. We might as well go home to luncheon.'

As we buttoned up our coats and started

back across the marsh, Jip ran ahead pretending he was looking for water rats.

'He knows something, all right,'
whispered the Doctor. 'And I think he knows
what has happened, too. It's funny, his not
wanting to tell me. He has never done that
before – not in eleven years. He has always
told me everything. Strange! Very strange!'

'Do you mean you think he knows all
about the Hermit, the big mystery about
him that folks hint at and all that?'

'I shouldn't wonder if he did,' the Doctor
answered slowly. 'I noticed something in his
expression the moment we found that door
open and the hut empty. And the way he
sniffed the floor too – it told him something,
that floor did. He saw signs we couldn't see.
I wonder why he won't tell me. I'll try him
again. Here, Jip! Jip! Where is the dog? I
thought he went on in front.'

'So did I,' I said. 'He was there a moment
ago. I saw him as large as life. Jip . . . Jip . . .
Jip . . . JIP!'

But he was gone. We called and called. We
even walked back to the hut. But Jip had
disappeared.

'Oh, well,' I said, 'most likely he has just
run home ahead of us. He often does that,

you know. We'll find him there when we get back to the house.'

But the Doctor just closed his coat collar tighter against the wind and strode on muttering, 'Odd – very odd!'

Chapter Three
JIP AND THE SECRET

WHEN we reached the house, the first question the Doctor asked of Dab-Dab in the hall was, 'Is Jip home yet?'

'No,' said Dab-Dab, 'I haven't seen him.'

'Let me know the moment he comes in, will you, please?' said the Doctor, hanging up his hat.

'Certainly I will,' said Dab-Dab. 'Don't be long over washing your hands; the lunch is on the table.'

Just as we were sitting down to luncheon in the kitchen we heard a great racket at the front door. I ran and opened it. In bounded Jip.

'Doctor!' he cried. 'Come into the library quick. I've got something to tell you. . . . No, Dab-Dab, the luncheon must wait. Please

hurry, Doctor. There's not a moment to be
lost. Don't let any of the animals come – just
you and Tommy.'

'Now,' he said, when we were in the
library and the door was closed, 'turn the
key in the lock and make sure there's no one
listening under the windows.'

'It's all right,' said the Doctor. 'Nobody can
hear you here. Now, what is it?'

'Well, Doctor,' said Jip (he was badly out of
breath from running), 'I know all about the
Hermit – I have known for years. But I
couldn't tell you.'

'Why?' asked the Doctor.

'Because I'd promised not to tell anyone. It
was Bob, his dog, that told me. And I swore
to him that I would keep the secret.'

'Well, are you going to tell me now?'

'Yes,' said Jip, 'we've got to save him. I
followed Bob's scent just now when I left you
out there on the marshes. And I found him.
And I said to him, "Is it all right," I said, "for
me to tell the Doctor now? Maybe he can do
something." And Bob says to me, "Yes," says
he, "it's all right because—"'

'Oh for heaven's sake, go on, go on!' cried
the Doctor. 'Tell us what the mystery is –
not what you said to Bob and what Bob said

to you. What has happened? Where *is* the Hermit?'

'He's in Puddleby Jail,' said Jip. 'He's in prison.'

'In prison!'

'Yes.'

'What for? What's he done?'

Jip went over to the door and smelled at the bottom of it to see if anyone was listening outside. Then he came back to the Doctor on tiptoe and whispered, *'He killed a man!'*

'Lord preserve us!' cried the Doctor, sitting down heavily in a chair and mopping his forehead with a handkerchief. 'When did he do it?'

'Fifteen years ago – in a Mexican gold mine. That's why he has been a hermit ever since. He shaved off his beard and kept away from people out there on the marshes so he wouldn't be recognized. But last week, it seems these newfangled policemen came to town, and they heard there was a strange man who kept to himself all alone in a shack on the fen. And they got suspicious. For a long time people had been hunting all over the world for the man that did the killing in the Mexican gold mine fifteen years ago.

So these policemen went out to the shack, and they recognized Luke by a mole on his arm. And they took him to prison.'

'Well, well!' murmured the Doctor. 'Who would have thought it? Luke, the philosopher! Killed a man! I can hardly believe it.'

'It's true enough – unfortunately,' said Jip. 'Luke did it. But it wasn't his fault. Bob says so. And he was there and saw it all. He was scarcely more than a puppy at the time. Bob says Luke couldn't help it. He *had* to do it.'

'Where is Bob now?' asked the Doctor.

'Down at the prison. I wanted him to come with me here to see you, but he won't leave the prison while Luke is there. He just sits outside the door of the prison cell and won't move. He doesn't even eat the food they give him. Won't you please come down there, Doctor, and see if there is anything you can do? The trial is to be this afternoon at two o'clock. What time is it now?'

'It's ten minutes past one.'

'Bob says he thinks they are going to kill Luke for a punishment if they can prove that he did it – or certainly keep him in prison for the rest of his life. Won't you please come? Perhaps if you spoke to the judge and told him what a good man Luke really is, they'd let him off.'

'Of course I'll come,' said the Doctor, getting up and moving to go. 'But I'm very much afraid that I shan't be of any help.' He turned at the door and hesitated thoughtfully.

'And yet . . . I wonder . . .'

Then he opened the door and passed out with Jip and me close at his heels.

Chapter Four
BOB

DAB-DAB was terribly upset when she found we were going away again without luncheon, and she made us take some cold pork pies in our pockets to eat on the way.

When we got to Puddleby Court-house (it was next door to the prison), we found a great crowd gathered around the building.

The news had run through the countryside that Luke the Hermit was to be tried for killing a man and that the great mystery, which had hung over him so long, was to be cleared up at last. The butcher and the baker had closed their shops and taken a holiday. All the farmers from round about and all the townfolk were there. I had never seen the quiet old town in such a state of excitement before.

If I hadn't had the Doctor with me I am sure I would never have been able to make my way through the mob packed around the court-house door. But I followed behind him, hanging on to his coat-tails, and at last we got safely into the jail.

'I want to see Luke,' said the Doctor to a very grand person in a blue coat with brass buttons standing at the door.

'Ask at the superintendent's office,' said the man. 'Third door on the left down the corridor.'

From there another policeman was sent with us to show us the way.

Outside the door of Luke's cell we found Bob, the bulldog, who wagged his tail sadly when he saw us. The man who was guiding us took a large bunch of keys from his pocket and opened the door.

I had never been inside a real prison cell before; and I felt quite a thrill when the policeman went out and locked the door after him, leaving us shut in the dimly-lighted little stone room. Before he went, he said that as soon as we had finished talking with our friend we should knock upon the door and he would come and let us out.

At first I could hardly see anything, it was

so dim inside. But after a little I made out a low bed against the wall, under a small barred window. On the bed, staring down at the floor between his feet, sat the Hermit, his head resting in his hands.

'Well, Luke,' said the Doctor in a kindly voice, 'they don't give you much light in here, do they?'

Very slowly the Hermit looked up from the floor.

'Hulloa, John Dolittle. What brings you here?'

'I've come to see you. I would have been here sooner, only I didn't hear about all this till a few minutes ago. I went to your hut to ask you if you would join me on a voyage, and when I found it empty I had no idea where you could be. I am dreadfully sorry to hear about your bad luck. I've come to see if there is anything I can do.'

Luke shook his head.

'No, I don't imagine there is anything can be done. They've caught me at last. That's the end of it, I suppose.'

He got up stiffly and started walking up and down the little room.

'In a way, I'm glad it's over,' said he. 'I never got any peace, always thinking they

'On the bed sat the Hermit'

were after me – afraid to speak to anyone.
They were bound to get me in the end. . . .
Yes, I'm glad it's over.'

Then the Doctor talked to Luke for more
than half an hour, trying to cheer him up,
while I sat around wondering what I ought
to say and wishing I could do something.

At last the Doctor said he wanted to see
Bob, and we knocked upon the door and
were let out by the policeman.

'Bob,' said the Doctor to the big bulldog in
the passage, 'come out with me to the porch.
I want to ask you something.'

'How is he, Doctor?' asked Bob as we
walked down the corridor into the court-
house porch.

'Oh, Luke's all right. Very miserable of
course, but he's all right. Now tell me, Bob:
You saw this business happen, didn't you?
You were there when the man was killed,
eh?'

'I was, Doctor,' said Bob, 'and I tell you—'

'All right,' the Doctor interrupted, 'that's
all I want to know for the present. There
isn't time to tell me more now. The trial is
just going to begin. There are the judge and
the lawyers coming up the steps. Now
listen, Bob: I want you to stay with me when

I go into the court-room. And whatever I tell you to do, do it. Do you understand? Don't make any scenes. Don't bite anybody, no matter what they may say about Luke. Just behave perfectly quietly and answer any question I may ask you – truthfully. Do you understand?'

'Very well. But do you think you will be able to get him off, Doctor?' asked Bob. 'He's a good man, Doctor. He really is. There never was a better.'

'We'll see, we'll see, Bob. It's a new thing I'm going to try. I'm not sure the judge will allow it. But . . . well, we'll see. It's time to go into the court-room now. Don't forget what I told you. Remember: for heaven's sake, don't start biting anyone or you'll get us all put out and spoil everything.'

Chapter Five
MENDOZA

INSIDE the court-room everything was very solemn and wonderful. It was a high, big room. Raised above the floor, against the wall was the judge's desk, and here the judge was already sitting – an old, handsome man in a marvellous big wig of grey hair and a gown of black. Below him was another wide, long desk at which lawyers in white wigs sat. The whole thing reminded me of a mixture between a church and a school.

'Those twelve people at the side,' whispered the Doctor – 'those in pews like a choir, they are what is called the jury. It is they who decide whether Luke is guilty – whether he did it or not.'

'And look!' I said. 'There's Luke himself in a sort of pulpit-thing with policemen each side of him. And there's another pulpit, the same kind, the other side of the room, see — only that one's empty.'

'That one is called the witness-box,' said the Doctor. 'Now I'm going down to speak to one of those men in white wigs, and I want you to wait here and keep these two seats for us. Bob will stay with you. Keep an eye on him — better hold on to his collar. I shan't be more than a minute or so.'

With that, the Doctor disappeared into the crowd that filled the main part of the room.

Then I saw the judge take up a funny little wooden hammer and knock on his desk with it. This, it seemed, was to make people keep quiet, for immediately everyone stopped buzzing and talking and began to listen very respectfully. Then another man in a black gown stood up and began reading from a paper in his hand.

He mumbled away exactly as though he were saying his prayers and didn't want anyone to understand what language they were in. But I managed to catch a few words:

'Biz...biz...biz...biz...biz...otherwise known as Luke the Hermit, of... biz ... biz...biz...biz... for killing his partner with...biz...biz...biz...otherwise known

as Bluebeard Bill on the night of the . . . *biz* . . .
biz . . . *biz* . . . in the *biz* . . . *biz* . . . *biz* . . .
of Mexico. Therefore Her Majesty's . . .
biz . . . *biz* . . . *biz* . . .'

At this moment I felt someone take hold of
my arm from the back, and turning round I
found the Doctor had returned with one of the
men in white wigs.

'Stubbins, this is Mr Percy Jenkyns,' said
the Doctor. 'He is Luke's lawyer. It is his
business to get Luke off – if he can.'

Mr Jenkyns seemed to be an extremely
young man with a round smooth face like a
boy. He shook hands with me and then
immediately turned and went on talking with
the Doctor.

'Oh, I think it is a perfectly precious idea,'
he was saying. 'Of *course* the dog must be
admitted as a witness; he was the only one
who saw the thing take place. I'm awfully glad
you came. I wouldn't have missed this for
anything. My hat! Won't it make the old court
sit up? This will stir things. A bulldog witness
for the defence! I do hope there are plenty of
reporters present. . . . Yes, there's one making
a sketch of the prisoner. I shall become known
after this. . . . And won't Conkey be pleased?
My hat!'

He put his hand over his mouth to smother a laugh and his eyes fairly sparkled with mischief.

'Who is Conkey?' I asked the Doctor.

'Sh! He is speaking of the judge up there, the Honourable Eustace Beauchamp Conckley.'

'Now,' said Mr Jenkyns, bringing out a note-book, 'tell me a little more about yourself, Doctor. You took your degree as Doctor of Medicine at Durham, I think you said. And the name of your last book was . . .?'

I could not hear any more for they talked in whispers, and I fell to looking round the court again.

Of course I could not understand everything that was going on, though it was all very interesting. People kept getting up in the place the Doctor called the witness-box, and the lawyers at the long table asked them questions about 'the night of the 29th.' Then the people would get down again and somebody else would get up and be questioned.

One of the lawyers (who, the Doctor told me afterwards, was called the prosecutor) seemed to be doing his best to get the Hermit into trouble by asking questions that made

it look as though he had always been a very
bad man. He was a nasty lawyer, this prosecutor, with a long nose.

Most of the time I could hardly keep my
eyes off poor Luke, who sat there between
his two policemen, staring at the floor as
though he weren't interested. The only time
I saw him take any notice at all was when
a small dark man with wicked little watery
eyes got up into the witness-box. I heard Bob
snarl under my chair as this person came
into the court-room and Luke's eyes just
blazed with anger and contempt.

This man said his name was Mendoza and
that he was the one who had guided the
Mexican police to the mine after Bluebeard
Bill had been killed. And at every word he
said I could hear Bob down below me
muttering between his teeth, 'It's a lie! It's
a lie! I'll chew his face! It's a lie!'

And both the Doctor and I had hard work
keeping the dog under the seat.

Then I noticed that our Mr Jenkyns had
disappeared from the Doctor's side. But
presently I saw him stand up at the long
table to speak to the judge.

'Your Honour,' said he, 'I wish to introduce
a new witness for the defence, Doctor John

Dolittle, the naturalist. Will you please step into the witness stand, Doctor?'

There was a buzz of excitement as the Doctor made his way across the crowded room, and I noticed the nasty lawyer with the long nose lean down and whisper something to a friend, smiling in an ugly way that made me want to pinch him.

Then Mr Jenkyns asked the Doctor a whole lot of questions about himself and made him answer in a loud voice so the whole court could hear. He finished up by saying, 'And you are prepared to swear, Doctor Dolittle, that you understand the language of dogs and can make them understand you. Is that so?'

'Yes,' said the Doctor, 'that is so.'

'And what, might I ask,' put in the judge in a very quiet dignified voice, 'has all this to do with the killing of – er, er, Bluebeard Bill?'

'This, Your Honour,' said Mr Jenkyns, talking in a very grand manner as though he were on a stage in a theatre. 'There is in this court-room at the present moment a bulldog, who was the only living thing that saw the man killed. With the court's permission I propose to put that dog in the witness box and have him questioned before you by the eminent scientist, Doctor John Dolittle.'

Chapter Six
THE JUDGE'S DOG

AT first there was a dead silence
in the court. Then everybody began whispering or giggling at the same time till the
whole room sounded like a great hive of
bees. Many people seemed to be shocked;
most of them were amused; and a few were
angry.

Presently up sprang the nasty lawyer
with the long nose.

'I protest, Your Honour,' he cried, waving
his arms wildly to the judge. 'I object. The
dignity of this court is in peril. I protest.'

'I am the one to take care of the dignity of
this court,' said the judge.

Then Mr Jenkyns got up again. (If it hadn't
been such a serious matter, it was almost like
a Punch-and-Judy show: somebody was

always popping down and somebody else popping up.)

'If there is any doubt on the score of our being able to do as we say, Your Honour will have no objection, I trust, to the Doctor's giving the court a demonstration of his powers – to show that he actually can understand the speech of animals?'

I thought I saw a twinkle of amusement come into the old judge's eyes as he sat considering a moment before he answered.

'No,' he said at last, 'I don't think so.' Then he turned to the Doctor.

'Are you quite sure you can do this?' he asked.

'Quite, Your Honour,' said the Doctor, ' – quite sure.'

'Very well, then,' said the judge. 'If you can satisfy us that you really are able to understand canine testimony, the dog shall be admitted as a witness. I do not see, in that case, how I could object to his being heard. But I warn you that if you are trying to make a laughing-stock of this court it will go hard with you.'

'I protest, I protest!' yelled the long-nosed prosecutor. 'This is a scandal, an outrage to the bar!'

'Sit down!' said the judge in a very stern voice.

'What animal does Your Honour wish me to talk with?' asked the Doctor.

'I would like you to talk to my own dog,' said the judge. 'He is outside in the cloakroom. I will have him brought in, and then we shall see what you can do.'

Then someone went out and fetched the judge's dog, a lovely great Russian wolf-hound with slender legs and a shaggy coat. He was a proud and beautiful creature.

'Now, Doctor,' said the judge, 'did you ever see this dog before? Remember, you are in the witness stand and under oath.'

'No, Your Honour, I never saw him before.'

'Very well, then, will you please ask him to tell you what I had for supper last night? He was with me and watched me while I ate.'

Then the Doctor and the dog started talking to one another in signs and sounds, and they kept at it for quite a long time.

And the Doctor began to giggle and get so interested that he seemed to forget all about the court and judge and everything else.

'What a time he takes!' I heard a fat woman in front of me whispering. 'He's only pretending. Of course he can't do it! Who ever heard of talking to a dog? He must think we're children.'

'Haven't you finished yet?' the judge asked the Doctor. 'It shouldn't take that long just to ask what I had for supper.'

'Oh, no, Your Honour,' said the Doctor. 'The dog told me that long ago. But then he went on to tell me what you did after supper.'

'Never mind that,' said the judge. 'Tell me what answer he gave you to my question.'

'He says you had a mutton chop, two baked potatoes, a pickled walnut, and a glass of ale.'

The Honorable Eustace Beauchamp Conckley went white to the lips.

'Sounds like witchcraft,' he muttered. 'I never dreamed—'

'And after your supper,' the Doctor went on, 'he says you went to see a prizefight and then sat up playing cards for money till twelve o'clock and came home singing, "We won't get—"'

'That will do,' the judge interrupted, 'I am satisfied you can do as you say. The prisoner's dog shall be admitted as a witness.'

'Sat scowling down upon the amazed and gaping jury'

'I protest, I object!' screamed the prosecutor. 'Your Honour, this is—'

'Sit down!' roared the judge. 'I say the dog shall be heard. That ends the matter. Put the witness in the stand.'

And then for the first time in the solemn history of England a dog was put in the witness box of Her Majesty's Court. And it was I, Tommy Stubbins (when the Doctor made a sign to me across the room), who proudly led Bob up the aisle, through the astonished crowd, past the frowning, spluttering, long-nosed prosecutor, and made him comfortable on a high chair in the witness-box; from where the old bulldog sat scowling down over the rail upon the amazed and gaping jury.

Chapter Seven
THE END OF THE MYSTERY

THE trial went swiftly forward after that. Mr Jenkyns told the Doctor to ask Bob what he saw on the night of the 29th, and when Bob had told all he knew and the Doctor had turned it into English for the judge and the jury, this was what he had to say:

'On the night of the 29th of November, 1824, I was with my master, Luke Fitzjohn (otherwise known as Luke the Hermit), and his two partners, Manuel Mendoza and William Boggs (otherwise known as Bluebeard Bill) in their gold mine in Mexico. For a long time these three men had been hunting for gold, and they had dug a deep hole in the ground. On the morning of the 29th gold was discovered, lots of it, at the bottom of this hole. And all three, my master and his two partners, were very happy about it because now they would be rich. But Manuel Mendoza asked Bluebeard Bill to go for a walk with him. These two men I had always suspected of being bad. So when I noticed that they left my master behind, I followed them secretly to see what they were up to. And in a deep cave in the mountains I heard them arrange together to kill Luke the Hermit so that they should get all the gold and he have none.'

At this point the judge asked, 'Where is the witness Mendoza? Constable, see that he does not leave the court.'

But the wicked little man with the watery eyes had already sneaked out when no one was looking, and he was never seen in Puddleby again.

'Then,' Bob's statement went on, 'I went to my master and tried very hard to make him understand that his partners were dangerous men. But it was no use. He did not understand dog language. So I did the next best thing: I never let him out of my sight but stayed with him every moment of the day and night.

'Now the hole that they had made was so

deep that to get down and up it you had to go in a bucket tied on the end of a rope, and the three men used to haul one another up and let one another down the mine in this way. That was how the gold was brought up, too – in the bucket. Well, about seven o'clock in the evening my master was standing at the top of the mine, hauling up Bluebeard Bill who was in the bucket. Just as he had got Bill halfway up I saw Mendoza come out of the hut where we all lived. Mendoza thought that Bill was away buying groceries. But he wasn't, he was in the bucket. And when Mendoza saw Luke hauling and straining on the rope, he thought he was pulling up a bucketful of gold. So he drew a pistol from his pocket and came sneaking up behind Luke to shoot him.

'I barked and barked to warn my master of the danger he was in, but he was so busy hauling up Bill (who was a heavy, fat man) that he took no notice of me. I saw that if I didn't do something quick he would surely be shot. So I did a thing I've never done before: suddenly and savagely I bit my master in the leg from behind. Luke was so hurt and startled that he did just what I wanted him to do: he let go the rope with

HUGH LOFTING

' "He drew a pistol and came sneaking up" '

both hands at once and turned round. And then – *crash!* – down went Bill in his bucket to the bottom of the mine and he was killed.

'While my master was busy scolding me Mendoza put his pistol in his pocket, came up with a smile on his face, and looked down the mine.

' "Why, good gracious!" said he to Luke. "You've killed Bluebeard Bill. I must go and tell the police" — hoping, you see, to get the whole mine to himself when Luke should be put in prison. Then he jumped on his horse and galloped away.

'And soon my master grew afraid, for he saw that if Mendoza only told enough lies to the police, it *would* look as though he had killed Bill on purpose. So while Mendoza was gone he and I stole away together secretly and came to England. Here he shaved off his beard and became a hermit. And ever since, for fifteen years, we've remained in hiding. This is all I have to say. And I swear it is the truth, every word.'

When the Doctor finished reading Bob's long speech the excitement among the twelve members of the jury was positively terrific. One, a very old man with white hair, began to weep in a loud voice at the thought of poor Luke hiding on the fen for fifteen years for something he couldn't help. And all the others set to whispering and nodding their heads to one another.

In the middle of all this up got that horrible prosecutor again, waving his arms more wildly than ever.

'Your Honour,' he cried. 'I must object to this evidence as biased. Of course the dog would not tell the truth against his own master. I object. I protest.'

'Very well,' said the judge, 'you are at liberty to cross-examine. It is your duty as prosecutor to prove his evidence untrue. There is the dog: question him, if you do not believe what he says.'

I thought the long-nosed lawyer would have a fit. He looked first at the dog, then at the Doctor, then at the judge, then back at the dog scowling from the witness-box. He opened his mouth to say something, but no words came. He waved his arms some more. His face got redder and redder. At last, clutching his forehead, he sank weakly into his seat and had to be helped out of the court-room by two friends. As he was half carried through the door he was still feebly murmuring, 'I protest . . . I object . . . I protest!'

Chapter Eight
THREE CHEERS

NEXT the judge made a very long speech to the jury, and when it was over all the members of the jury got up and went out into the next room. And at that point the Doctor came back, leading Bob, to the seat beside me.

'What have the jury gone out for?' I asked.

'They always do that at the end of a trial, to make up their minds whether the prisoner did it or not.'

'Couldn't you and Bob go in with them and help them make up their minds the right way?' I asked.

'No, that's not allowed. They have to talk it over in secret. Sometimes it takes . . . my gracious look, they're coming back already! They didn't spend long over it.'

Everybody kept quite still while the twelve jurors came tramping back into their places in the pews. Then one of the them, the leader – a little man – stood up and turned to the judge. Everyone was holding his breath, especially the Doctor and myself, to see what he was going to say. You could have heard a pin drop while the whole court-room, the whole of Puddleby in fact, waited with craning necks and straining ears to hear the weighty words.

'Your Honour,' said the little man, 'the jury returns a verdict of *Not Guilty.*'

'What's that mean?' I asked, turning to the Doctor.

But I found Doctor John Dolittle, the famous naturalist, standing on top of a chair, dancing about on one leg like a schoolboy.

'It means he's free!' he cried. 'Luke is free!'

'Then he'll be able to come on the voyage with us, won't he?'

But I could not hear his answer, for the whole court-room seemed to be jumping up on chairs like the Doctor. The crowd had suddenly gone crazy. All the people were laughing and calling and waving to Luke to show him how glad they were that he was free. The noise was deafening.

Then it stopped. All was quiet again, and the people stood up respectfully while the judge left the court. For the trial of Luke the Hermit, that famous trial which to this day they are still talking of in Puddleby, was over.

In the hush while the judge was leaving, a sudden shriek rang out, and there in the doorway stood a woman, her arms outstretched to the Hermit.

'Luke!' she cried, 'I've found you at last!'

'It's his wife,' the fat woman in front of me whispered. 'She ain't seen 'im in fifteen years, poor dear! What a lovely reunion. I'm glad I came. I wouldn't have missed this for anything!'

As soon as the judge had gone the noise broke out again, and now the folks gathered round Luke and his wife and shook them by the hand and congratulated them and laughed over them and cried over them.

'Come along, Stubbins,' said the Doctor, taking me by the arm, 'let's get out of this while we can.'

'But aren't you going to speak to Luke?' I said – 'to ask him if he'll come on the voyage?'

'It wouldn't be a bit of use, said the Doctor.

'His wife's come for him. No man stands any chance of going on a voyage when his wife hasn't seen him in fifteen years. Come along. Let's get home to tea. We didn't have any lunch, remember. And we've earned something to eat. We'll have one of those mixed meals, lunch and tea combined – with watercress and ham. Nice change. Come along.'

Just as we were going to step out at a side door I heard the crowd shouting, 'The Doctor! The Doctor! Where's the Doctor? The Hermit would have hanged if it hadn't been for the Doctor. Speech! Speech! The Doctor!'

And a man came running up to us and said, 'The people are calling for you sir.'

'I'm very sorry,' said the Doctor, 'but I'm in a hurry.'

'The crowd won't be denied, sir,' said the man. 'They want you to make a speech in the market-place.'

'Beg them to excuse me,' said the Doctor –'with my compliments. I have an appointment at my house – a very important one that I may not break. Tell Luke to make a speech. Come along, Stubbins, this way.'

'Oh, Lord!' he muttered as we got out into

the open air and found another crowd
waiting for him at the side door. 'Let's go up
that alleyway to the left. Quick! Run!'

We took to our heels, darted through a
couple of side streets and just managed to
get away from the crowd.

It was not till we had gained the
Oxenthorpe Road that we dared to slow
down to a walk and take our breath. And
even when we reached the Doctor's gate and
turned to look backwards towards the town,
the faint murmur of many voices still
reached us on the evening wind.

'They're still clamouring for you,' I said.
'Listen!'

The murmur suddenly swelled up into a
low distant roar, and although it was a mile
and half away you could distinctly hear the
words:

'Three cheers for Luke the Hermit:
Hooray! – Three cheers for his dog: Hooray!
– Three cheers for his wife: Hooray! –
Three cheers for the Doctor: Hooray!
Hooray! HOO-R-A-Y!'

Chapter Nine
THE PURPLE
BIRD OF PARADISE

POLYNESIA was waiting for us on the front porch. She looked full of some important news.

'Doctor,' said she, 'the purple bird of paradise has arrived!'

'At last!' said the Doctor. 'I had begun to fear some accident had befallen her. And how is Miranda?'

From the excited way in which the Doctor fumbled his key into the lock, I guessed that we were not going to get our tea right away, even now.

'Oh, she seemed all right when she arrived,' said Polynesia – 'tired from her long journey, of course, but otherwise all right. But what *do* you think? That mischief-making sparrow, Cheapside, insulted her as soon as she came into the garden. When I arrived on the scene she was in tears and was all for turning round and going straight back to Brazil tonight. I had the hardest work persuading her to wait till you came. She's in the study. I shut Cheapside in one of your bookcases and told him I'd tell you exactly what had happened the moment you got home.'

The Doctor frowned, then walked silently and quickly to the study.

Here we found the candles lit, for the daylight was nearly gone. Dab-Dab was standing on the floor mounting guard over one of the glass-fronted bookcases in which Cheapside had been imprisoned. The noisy little sparrow was still fluttering angrily behind the glass when we came in.

In the centre of the big table, perched on the inkstand, stood the most beautiful bird I have ever seen. She had a deep violet-coloured breast, scarlet wings, and a long, long, sweeping tail of gold. She was unimaginably beautiful but looked dreadfully tired. Already she had her head under her wing, and she swayed gently from side to side on top of the inkstand like a bird that has flown long and far.

'Sh!' said Dab-Dab. 'Miranda is asleep. I've got this little imp Cheapside in here. Listen, Doctor, for heaven's sake send that sparrow away before he does any more mischief. He's nothing but a vulgar little nuisance. We've had a perfectly awful time trying to get Miranda to stay. Shall I serve your tea in here, or will you come into the kitchen when you're ready?'

'We'll come into the kitchen, Dab-Dab,' said the Doctor. 'Let Cheapside out before you go, please.'

Dab-Dab opened the bookcase door and Cheapside strutted out trying hard not to look guilty.

'Cheapside,' said the Doctor sternly, 'what did you say to Miranda when she arrived?'

'I didn't say nothing, Doc, straight I didn't. That is, nothing much. I was picking up crumbs off the gravel path when she comes swanking into the garden, turning up her nose in all directions, as though she owned the earth — just because she's got a lot of coloured plumage. A London sparrow's as good as her any day. I don't hold by these gaudy, bedizened foreigners, nohow. Why don't they stay in their own country?'

'But what did you say to her that got her
so offended?'

'All I said was, "You don't belong in an
English garden; you ought to be in a
milliner's window." That's all.'

'You ought to be ashamed of yourself,
Cheapside. Don't you realize that this bird
has come thousands of miles to see me —
only to be insulted by your impertinent
tongue as soon as she reaches my garden?
What do you mean by it? If she had gone
away again before I got back tonight, I
would never have forgiven you. Leave the
room.'

Sheepishly, but still trying to look as
though he didn't care, Cheapside hopped out
into the passage and Dab-Dab closed the
door.

The Doctor went up to the beautiful bird
on the inkstand and gently stroked its back.
Instantly, its head popped out from under
its wing.

Chapter Ten
LONG ARROW,
THE SON OF GOLDEN ARROW

'**W**ELL, Miranda,' said the Doctor. 'I'm terribly sorry this has happened. But you mustn't mind Cheapside; he doesn't know any better. He's a city bird, and all his life he has had to squabble for a living. You must make allowances. He doesn't know any better.'

Miranda stretched her gorgeous wings wearily. Now that I saw her awake and moving, I noticed what a superior, well bred manner she had. There were tears in her eyes and her beak was trembling.

'I wouldn't have minded so much,' she said in a high silvery voice, 'if I hadn't been so dreadfully worn out. . . . That and something else,' she added beneath her breath.

'Did you have a hard time getting here?' asked the Doctor.

'The worst passage I ever made,' said Miranda. 'The weather – well there! What's the use? I'm here anyway.'

'Tell me,' said the Doctor as though he had been impatiently waiting to say something for a long time, 'what did Long Arrow say when you gave him my message?'

The purple bird of paradise hung her head.

'That's the worst part of it,' she said. 'I might almost as well have not come at all. I wasn't able to deliver your message. I couldn't find him. *Long Arrow, the son of Golden Arrow, has disappeared!'*

'Disappeared!' cried the Doctor. 'Why, what's become of him?'

'Nobody knows,' Miranda answered. 'He had often disappeared before, as I have told you – so that the Indians didn't know where he was. But it's a mighty hard thing to hide away from the birds. I had always been able to find some owl or martin who could tell me where he was, if I wanted to know. But not this time. That's why I'm nearly a fortnight late in coming to you: I kept hunting and hunting, asking everywhere. I went over

the whole length and breadth of South
America. But there wasn't a living thing
could tell me where he was.'

There was a sad silence in the room after
she had finished; the Doctor was frowning
in a peculiar sort of way and Polynesia
scratched her head.

'Did you ask the black parrots?' asked
Polynesia. 'They usually know everything.'

'Certainly I did,' said Miranda. 'And I was
so upset at not being able to find out anything
that I forgot all about observing the weather
signs before I started my flight here. I didn't
even bother to break my journey at the
Azores, but cut right across, making for the
Strait of Gibraltar – as though it were June
or July. And of course I ran into a perfectly
frightful storm in mid-Atlantic. I really
thought I'd never come through it. Luckily
I found a piece of a wrecked vessel floating
in the sea after the storm had partly died
down, and I roosted on it and took some sleep.
If I hadn't been able to take that rest, I
wouldn't be here to tell the tale.'

'Poor Miranda! What a time you must
have had!' said the Doctor. 'But tell me, were
you able to find out whereabouts Long
Arrow was last seen?'

'Yes. A young albatross told me he had seen him on Spider Monkey Island.'

'Spider Monkey Island? That's somewhere off the coast of Brazil, isn't it?'

'Yes, that's it. Of course I flew there right away and asked every bird on the island — and it is a big island, a hundred miles long. It seems that Long Arrow was visiting some peculiar Indians that live there, and that when last seen he was going up into the mountains looking for rare medicine plants. I got that from a tame hawk, a pet, which the Chief of the Indians keeps for hunting partridges with. I nearly got caught and put in a cage for my pains, too. That's the worst of having beautiful feathers: it's as much as your life is worth to go near most humans. They say, "Oh, how pretty!" and shoot an arrow or a bullet into you. You and Long Arrow were the only two men that I would ever trust myself near — out of all the people in the world.'

'But was he never known to have returned from the mountains?'

'No. That was the last that was seen or heard of him. I questioned the seabirds around the shores to find out if he had left the island in a canoe. But they could tell me nothing.'

'Do you think that some accident has happened to him?' asked the Doctor in a fearful voice.

'I'm afraid it must have,' said Miranda shaking her head.

'Well,' said John Dolittle slowly, 'if I could never meet Long Arrow face to face it would be the greatest disappointment in my whole life. Not only that, but it would be a great loss to the knowledge of the human race. For, from what you have told me of him, he knew more natural science than all the rest of us put together; and if he has gone without anyone to write it down for him so the world may be the better for it, it would be a terrible thing. But you don't really think that he is dead, do you?'

'What else can I think,' asked Miranda, bursting into tears, 'when for six whole months he has not been seen by flesh, fish, or fowl.'

' "What else can I think?" '

Chapter Eleven
BLIND TRAVEL

THIS news about Long Arrow made us all very sad. And I could see from the silent dreamy way the Doctor took his tea that he was dreadfully upset. Every once in a while he would stop eating altogether and sit staring at the spots on the kitchen table-cloth as though his thoughts were far away, till Dab-Dab, who was watching to see that he got a good meal, would cough or rattle the pots in the sink.

I did my best to cheer him up by reminding him of all he had done for Luke and his wife that afternoon. And when that didn't seem to work, I went on talking about our preparations for the voyage.

'But you see, Stubbins,' said he as we rose from the table and Dab-Dab and Chee-Chee began to clear away, 'I don't know where to go now. I feel sort of lost since Miranda brought me this news. On this voyage I had planned going to see Long Arrow. I had been looking forward to it for a whole year. I felt he might help me in learning the language of the shellfish – and perhaps in finding some way of getting to the bottom of the sea. But now? He's gone! And all his great knowledge has gone with him.'

Then he seemed to fall a-dreaming again.

'Just to think of it!' he murmured. 'Long Arrow and I, two students. Although I'd never met him, I felt as though I knew him quite well. For, in his way – without any schooling – he has all his life been trying to do the very things that I have tried to do in mine. And now he's gone! A whole world lay between us – and only a bird knew us both!'

We went back into the study, where Jip brought the Doctor his slippers and his pipe. And after the pipe was lit and the smoke began to fill the room the old man seemed to cheer up a little.

'But you will go on some voyage, Doctor, won't you?' I asked, 'even if you can't go to find Long Arrow.'

He looked up sharply into my face, and I

suppose he saw how anxious I was. Because he suddenly smiled his old, boyish smile and said, 'Yes, Stubbins. Don't worry. We'll go. We mustn't stop working and learning, even if poor Long Arrow has disappeared. But where to go: that's the question. Where shall we go?'

There were so many places that I wanted to go that I couldn't make up my mind right away. And while I was still thinking, the Doctor sat up in his chair and said, 'I tell you what we'll do, Stubbins: it's a game I used to play when I was young – before Sarah came to live with me. I used to call it Blind Travel. Whenever I wanted to go on a voyage and I couldn't make up my mind where to go, I would take the atlas and open it with my eyes shut. Next, I'd wave a pencil, still without looking, and stick it down on whatever page had fallen open. Then I'd open my eyes and look. It's a very exciting game, is Blind Travel. Because you have to swear before you begin that you will go to the place the pencil touches, come what may. Shall we play it?'

'Oh, let's!' I almost yelled. 'How thrilling! I hope it's China . . . or Borneo . . . or Baghdad.'

And in a moment I had scrambled up the bookcase, dragged the big atlas from the top shelf, and laid it on the table before the Doctor.

I knew every page in that atlas by heart. How many days and nights I had lingered over its faded maps, following the blue rivers from the mountains to the sea, wondering what the little towns really looked like and how wide were the sprawling lakes!

As the Doctor began sharpening his pencil a thought came to me.

'What if the pencil falls upon the North Pole?' I asked. 'Will we have to go there?'

'No. The rules of the game say you don't have to go to any place you've been to before. You are allowed another try. I've been to the North Pole,' he ended quietly, 'so we shan't have to go there.'

I could hardly speak with astonishment.

'You've been to the North Pole!' I managed to gasp out at last. 'But I thought it was still undiscovered. The map shows all the places explorers have reached *trying* to get there. Why isn't your name down if you discovered it?'

'I promised to keep it a secret. And you must promise me never to tell anyone. Yes,

I discovered the North Pole in April, 1809.
But shortly after I got there the polar bears
came to me in a body and told me there was
a great deal of coal there, buried beneath
the snow. They knew, they said, that human
beings would do anything and go anywhere
to get coal. So would I please keep it a secret.
Because once people began coming up there
to start coal mines, their beautiful white
country would be spoiled – and there was
nowhere else in the world cold enough for
polar bears to be comfortable. So of course I
had to promise them I would. Ah, well, it
will be discovered again some day, by somebody else. But I want the polar bears to have
their playground to themselves as long as
possible. And I daresay it will be a good
while yet, for it certainly is a fiendish place
to get to. Well, now, are we ready? Good!
Take the pencil and stand here close to the
table. When the book falls open, wave the
pencil around three times and jab it down.
Ready? All right, shut your eyes.'

It was a tense and fearful moment – but
very thrilling. We both had our eyes shut
tight. I heard the atlas fall open with a bang.
I wondered what page it was: England or
Asia. If it should be the map of Asia, so

'It was a tense and fearful moment'

much would depend on where that pencil would land. I waved three times in a circle. I began to lower my hand. The pencil point touched the page.

'All right,' I called out, 'it's done.'

Chapter Twelve
DESTINY AND DESTINATION

WE both opened our eyes, then bumped our heads together with a crack, in our eagerness to lean over and see where we were to go.

The atlas lay open at a map called *Chart of the South Atlantic Ocean*. My pencil point was resting right in the centre of a tiny island. The name of it was printed so small that the Doctor had to get out his strong spectacles to read it. I was trembling with excitement.

'*Spider Monkey Island,*' he read out slowly. Then he whistled softly beneath his breath. 'Of all the extraordinary things! You've hit upon the very island where Long Arrow was last seen on earth. I wonder . . . Well, well! How very singular!'

'We'll go there, Doctor, won't we?' I asked.

'Of course we will. The rules of the game say we've got to.'

'I'm so glad it wasn't Oxenthorpe or Bristol,' I said. 'It'll be a grand voyage, this. Look at all the sea we've got to cross. Will it take us long?'

'Oh, no,' said the Doctor, – 'not very. With a good boat and a good wind we should make it easily in four weeks. But isn't it extra-ordinary? Of all the places in the world you picked out that one with your eyes shut. Spider Monkey Island after all! – Well, there's one good thing about it: I shall be able to get some jabizri beetles.'

'What are jabizri beetles?'

'They are a very rare kind of beetle with peculiar habits. I want to study them. There are only three countries in the world where they are to be found. Spider Monkey Island is one of them. But even there they are very scarce.'

'What is this little question mark after the name of the island for?' I asked, pointing to the map.

'That means that the island's position in the ocean is not known very exactly – that it is somewhere *about* there. Ships have probably seen it in that neighbourhood, that is all, most likely. It is quite possible we shall be the first to land there. But I daresay we shall have some difficulty in finding it first.'

How like a dream it all sounded! The two of us sitting there at the big study table, the candles lit, the smoke curling towards the dim ceiling from the Doctor's pipe – the two of us sitting there, talking about finding an island in the ocean and being the first Europeans to land upon it!

'I'll bet it will be a great voyage,' I said. 'It looks a lovely island on the map. Will there be natives there?'

'A peculiar tribe of Indians lives on it, Miranda tells me.'

At this point the poor bird of paradise stirred and woke up. In our excitement we had forgotten to speak low.

'We are going to Spider Monkey Island, Miranda,' said the Doctor. 'You know where it is, do you not?'

'I know where it was the last time I saw it,' said the bird. 'But whether it will be there still, I can't say.'

'What do you mean?' asked the Doctor. 'It is always in the same place, surely?'

'Not by any means,' said Miranda. 'Why, didn't you know? Spider Monkey Island is a *floating* island. It moves around all over the place – usually somewhere near southern South America. But of course I could surely find it for you, if you want to go there.'

At this fresh piece of news I could contain myself no longer. I was bursting to tell someone. I ran dancing and singing from the room to find Chee-Chee.

At the door I tripped over Dab-Dab, who was just coming in with her wings full of plates, and fell headlong on my nose.

'Has the boy gone crazy?' cried the duck. 'Where do you think you're going, ninny?'

'To Spider Monkey Island!' I shouted, picking myself up and doing cartwheels down the hall. 'Spider Monkey Island! Hooray! . . . And it's a *floating* island!'

'You're going to Bedlam, I should say,' snorted the housekeeper. 'Look what you've done to my best china!'

But I was far too happy to listen to her scolding, and I ran on, singing, into the kitchen to find Chee-Chee.

PART III

Chapter One
THE THIRD MAN

THAT same week we began our preparations for the voyage.

Joe, the mussel man, had *The Curlew* moved down the river and tied it up along the river wall, so it would be more handy for loading. And for three whole days we carried provisions down to our beautiful new boat and stowed them away.

I was surprised to find how roomy and big she was inside. There were three little cabins, a saloon (or dining room), and underneath all this, a big place called the hold, where the food and extra sails and other things were kept.

I think Joe must have told everybody in the town about our coming voyage because there was always a regular crowd watching us when we brought the things down to put aboard. And of course, sooner or later, old Matthew Mugg was bound to turn up.

'My goodness, Tommy,' said he, as he watched me carrying on some sacks of flour, 'but that's a pretty boat! Where might the Doctor be going to this voyage?'

'We're going to Spider Monkey Island,' I said proudly.

'And be you the only one the Doctor's taking along?'

'Well, he has spoken of wanting to take another man,' I said, 'but so far he hasn't made up his mind.'

Matthew grunted, then squinted up at the graceful masts of *The Curlew*.

'You know, Tommy,' said he 'if it wasn't for my rheumatism I've half a mind to come with the doctor myself. There's something about a boat standing ready to sail that always did make me feel venturesome and travellish-like. What's the stuff in the cans you're taking on?'

'This is treacle,' I said – 'twenty pounds of treacle.'

'My goodness,' he sighed, turning away sadly. 'That makes me feel more like going with you than ever. But my rheumatism is that bad I can't hardly—'

I didn't hear any more, for Matthew had moved off, still mumbling, into the crowd that stood about the wharf. The clock in Puddleby Church struck noon and I turned back, feeling very busy and important, to the task of loading.

But it wasn't very long before someone else came along and interrupted my work. This was a huge, big burly man with a red beard and tattoo marks all over his arms. He wiped his mouth with the back of his hand, spat twice on to the river wall and said, 'Boy, where's the skipper?'

'The *skipper*! . . . Who do you mean?' I asked.

'The captain. . . . Where's the captain of this craft?' he said, pointing to *The Curlew*.

'Oh, you mean the Doctor,' said I. 'Well, he isn't here at present.'

At that moment the Doctor arrived with his arms full of notebooks and butterfly nets and glass cases and other natural history things. The big man went up to him, respectfully touching his cap.

'Good morning, Captain,' said he. 'I heard

' "Boy, where's the skipper?" '

you was in need of hands for a voyage. My
name's Ben Butcher, able seaman.'

'I am very glad to know you,' said the
Doctor. 'But I'm afraid I shan't be able to
take on any more crew.'

'Why, but Captain,' said the able seaman,
'you surely ain't going to face deep-sea
weather with nothing more than this bit of
a lad to help you – and with a cutter that
big!'

The Doctor assured him that he was, but
the man didn't go away. He hung around
and argued. He told us he had known of
many ships being sunk through 'under-
manning'. He got out what he called his
stiffikit – a paper which said what a good
sailor he was – and implored us, if we
valued our lives, to take him on.

The Doctor was quite firm – polite but
determined – and finally the man walked
sorrowfully away, telling us he never
expected to see us alive again.

Callers of one sort and another kept us
quite busy that morning. The Doctor had no
sooner gone below to stow away his
notebooks than another visitor appeared
upon the gangplank. This was a black man,
very fashionably dressed.

'Pardon me,' said he, bowing elegantly, 'but is this the ship of the physician Dolittle?'

'Yes,' I said, 'did you wish to see him?'

'I did – if it will not be discommodious,' he answered.

'Who shall I say it is?'

'I am Bumpo Kahbooboo, Crown Prince of Jolliginki.'

I ran downstairs at once and told the Doctor.

'How fortunate! cried John Dolittle. 'My old friend Bumpo! Well, well! He's studying at Oxford, you know. How good of him to come all this way to call on me!' And he tumbled up the ladder to greet his visitor.

The man seemed to be overcome with joy when the Doctor appeared and shook him warmly by the hand.

'News reached me,' he said, 'that you were about to sail upon a voyage. I hastened to see you before your departure. I am sublimely ecstasied that I did not miss you.'

'You very nearly did miss us,' said the Doctor. 'As it happened, we were delayed somewhat in getting the necessary number of men to sail our boat. If it hadn't been for that, we would have been gone three days ago.'

'How many men does your ship's company yet require?' asked Bumpo.

'Only one,' said the Doctor – 'but it is so hard to find the right one.'

'Methinks I detect something of the finger of Destination in this,' said Bumpo. 'How would I do?'

'Splendidly,' said the Doctor. 'But what about your studies? You can't very well just go off and leave your university career to take care of itself, you know.'

'I need a holiday,' said Bumpo. 'Even had I not gone with you, I intended at the end of this term to take a three-months' absconsion. But besides, I shall not be neglecting my education if I accompany you. Before I left Jolliginki my august father, the King, told me to be sure and travel plenty. You are a man of great studiosity. To see the world in your company is an opportunity not to be sneezed upon. No, no, indeed.'

'How did you like the life at Oxford?' asked the Doctor.

'Oh, passably, passably,' said Bumpo. 'I liked it all except the algebra and the shoes. The algebra hurt my head and the shoes hurt my feet. I threw the shoes over a wall as soon as I got out of the college

quadrilateral this morning, and the algebra
I am happily forgetting very fast. I liked
Cicero — yes, I think Cicero's fine — so
simultaneous. By the way, they tell me his
son is rowing for our college next year —
charming fellow.'

The Doctor looked down at the man's huge
bare feet thoughtfully a moment.

'Well,' he said slowly, 'there is something
in what you say, Bumpo, about getting education from the world as well as from the college. And if you are really sure that you
want to come, we shall be delighted to have
you. Because, to tell you the truth, I think
you are exactly the man we need.'

Chapter Two
GOOD-BYE!

TWO days after that we had all in readiness for our departure.

On this voyage Jip begged so hard to be taken that the Doctor finally gave in and said he could come. Polynesia and Chee-Chee were the only other animals to go with us. Dab-Dab was left in charge of the house and the animal family we were to leave behind.

Of course, as is always the way, at the last moment we kept remembering things we had forgotten, and when we finally closed the house up and went down the steps to the street, we were all burdened with armfuls of odd packages.

Halfway to the river, the Doctor suddenly remembered that he had left the stockpot boiling on the kitchen fire. However, we saw a blackbird flying by who nested in our garden, and the Doctor asked her to go back for us and tell Dab-Dab about it.

Down at the river wall we found a great crowd waiting to see us off.

Standing right near the gangplank were my mother and father. I hoped that they would not make a scene or burst into tears, or anything like that. But as a matter of fact they behaved quite well – for parents. My mother said something about being sure not to get my feet wet; and my father just smiled a crooked sort of smile, patted me on the back, and wished me luck.

We were a little surprised not to see Matthew Mugg among the crowd. We had felt sure that he would be there, and the Doctor had intended to give him some extra instructions about the food for the animals we had left at the house.

At last, after much pulling and tugging, we got the anchor up and undid a lot of mooring ropes. Then *The Curlew* began to move gently down the river with the out-running tide, while the people on the wall cheered and waved their handkerchiefs.

We bumped into one or two other boats

getting out into the stream, and at one sharp bend in the river we got stuck on a mudbank for a few minutes. But though the people on the shore seemed to get excited at these things, the Doctor did not appear to be disturbed by them in the least.

'These little accidents will happen in the most carefully regulated voyages,' he said as he leaned over the side and fished for his boots, which had got stuck in the mud while we were pushing off. 'Sailing is much easier when you get out into the open sea. There aren't so many silly things to bump into.'

For me indeed it was a great and wonderful feeling, that getting out into the open sea, when at length we passed the little lighthouse at the mouth of the river and found ourselves free of the land. It was all so new and different: just the sky above you and sea below. This ship, which was to be our house and our street, our home and our garden, for so many days to come, seemed so tiny in all this wide water – so tiny and yet so snug, sufficient, safe.

I looked around me and took a deep breath. The Doctor was at the wheel steering the boat which was now leaping and plunging gently through the waves. (I had expected to feel seasick at first but was delighted to find that I didn't.) Bumpo had been told to go downstairs and prepare dinner for us. Chee-Chee was coiling up ropes in the stern and laying them in neat piles. My work was fastening down the things on the deck so that nothing could roll about if the weather should grow rough when we got farther from the land. Jip was up in the peak of the boat with his ears cocked and nose stuck out – like a statue, so still – his keen old eyes keeping a sharp lookout for floating wrecks, sandbars, and other dangers. Each one of us had some special job to do, part of the proper running of a ship. Even old Polynesia was taking the sea's temperature with the Doctor's bath thermometer tied on the end of a string, to make sure there were no icebergs near us. As I listened to her swearing softly to herself because she couldn't read the pesky figures in the fading light, I realized that the voyage had begun in earnest and that very soon it would be night – my first night at sea!

Chapter Three
OUR TROUBLES BEGIN

JUST before suppertime Bumpo appeared from downstairs and went to the Doctor at the wheel.

'A stowaway in the hold, sir,' said he in a very business-like seafaring voice. 'I just discovered him, behind the flour bags.'

'Dear me!' said the Doctor. 'What a nuisance! Stubbins, go down with Bumpo and bring the man up. I can't leave the wheel just now.'

So Bumpo and I went down into the hold; and there, behind the flour bags, plastered in flour from head to foot, we found a man. After we had swept most of the flour off him with a broom, we discovered that it was Matthew Mugg. We hauled him upstairs sneezing and took him before the Doctor.

'Why, Matthew!' said John Dolittle. 'What on earth are you doing here?'

'The temptation was too much for me, Doctor,' said the cat's-meat man. 'You know I've often asked you to take me on voyages with you and you never would. Well, this time, knowing that you needed an extra man, I thought if I stayed hid till the ship was well at sea you would find I came in handy-like and keep me. But I had to lie so doubled up for hours behind them flour bags that my rhematism came on something awful. I just had to change my position, and of course just as I stretched out my legs, along comes this here African cook of yours and sees my feet sticking out. . . . Don't this ship roll something awful! How long has this storm been going on? I reckon this damp sea air wouldn't be very good for my rheumatics.'

'No, Matthew, it really isn't. You ought not to have come. You are not in any way suited to this kind of a life. I'm sure you wouldn't enjoy a long voyage a bit. We'll stop in at Penzance and put you ashore. Bumpo, please go downstairs to my bunk, and, listen, in the pocket of my dressing gown you'll find some maps. Bring me the small one – with blue pencil marks at the top. I know Penzance is over here on our left somewhere. But I must find out what light-houses there are before I change the ship's course and sail inshore.'

'Very good, sir,' said Bumpo, turning round smartly and making for the stairway.

'Now, Matthew,' said the Doctor, 'you can take the coach from Penzance to Bristol. And from there it is not very far to Puddleby, as you know. Don't forget to take the usual provisions to the house every Thursday, and be particularly careful to remember the extra supply of herring for the baby minks.'

While we were waiting for the maps Chee-Chee and I set about lighting the lamps: a green one on the right side of the ship, a red one on the left, and a white one on the mast.

At last we heard someone trundling on the stairs again and the Doctor said, 'Ah, here's Bumpo with the maps at last!'

But to our astonishment it was not Bumpo alone that appeared but *three* people.

'Good Lord, deliver us! Who are these?' cried John Dolittle.

'Two more stowaways, sir,' said Bumpo, stepping forward briskly. 'I found them in your cabin hiding under the bunk. One woman and one man, sir. Here are the maps.'

'This is too much,' said the Doctor feebly. 'Who are they? I can't see their faces in this dim light. Strike a match, Bumpo.'

You could never guess who it was. It was Luke and his wife. Mrs Luke appeared to be very miserable and seasick.

They explained to the Doctor that after they had settled down to live together in the little shack out on the fens, so many people came to visit them (having heard about the great trial) that life became impossible; and they had decided to escape from Puddleby in this manner – for they had no money to leave any other way – and try to find some new place to live where they and their story wouldn't be so well known. But as soon as the ship had begun to roll Mrs Luke had got most dreadfully unwell.

Poor Luke apologized many times for being such a nuisance and said that the whole thing had been his wife's idea.

The Doctor, after he had sent below for his medicine bag and had given Mrs Luke some *sal volatile* and smelling salts, said he thought the best thing to do would be for him to lend them some money and put them ashore at Penzance with Matthew. He also wrote a letter for Luke to take with him to a friend the Doctor had in the town of Penzance who, it was hoped, would be able to find Luke work to do there.

As the Doctor opened his purse and took out some gold coins I heard Polynesia, who was sitting on my shoulder watching the whole affair, mutter beneath her breath, 'There he goes – lending his last blessed penny – three pounds ten – all the money we had for the whole trip! Now we haven't the price of a postage stamp aboard if we should lose an anchor or have to buy a pint of tar. Well, let's pray we don't run out of food. Why doesn't he give them the ship and walk home?'

Presently with the help of the map the course of the boat was changed and, to Mrs Luke's great relief, we made for Penzance and dry land.

I was tremendously interested to see how a ship could be steered into a port at night with nothing but lighthouses and a compass to guide you. It seemed to me that the Doctor missed all the rocks and sandbars very cleverly.

We got into that funny little Cornish harbour about eleven o'clock that night. The Doctor took his stowaways on shore in our small rowboat, which we kept on the deck of *The Curlew*, and found them rooms at the hotel there. When he got back he told us that Mrs Luke had gone straight to bed and was feeling much better.

It was now after midnight, so we decided to stay in the harbour and wait till morning before setting out again.

I was glad to get to bed, although I felt that staying up so tremendously late was great fun. As I climbed into the bunk over the Doctor's and pulled the blankets snugly around me, I found I could look out of the porthole at my elbow, and, without raising my head from the pillow, could see the lights of Penzance swinging gently up and down with the motion of the ship at anchor. It was like being rocked to sleep with a little show going on to amuse you. I was just deciding that I liked the life of the sea very much when I fell fast asleep.

Chapter Four
OUR TROUBLES CONTINUE

THE next morning when we were eating a very excellent breakfast of kidneys and bacon, prepared by our good cook Bumpo, the Doctor said to me, 'I was just wondering, Stubbins, whether I should stop at the Capa Blanca Islands or run right across for the coast of Brazil. Miranda said we could expect a spell of excellent weather now — for four and a half weeks at least.'

'Well,' I said, spooning out the sugar at the bottom of my cocoa cup, 'I should think it would be best to make straight across while we are sure of good weather. And, besides, the purple bird of paradise is going to keep a look-out for us, isn't she? She'll be wondering what's happened to us if we don't get there in about a month.'

'True, quite true, Stubbins. On the other hand, the Capa Blancas make a very convenient stopping place on our way across. If we should need supplies or repairs, it would be very handy to put in there.'

'How long will it take us from here to the Capa Blancas?' I asked.

'About six days,' said the Doctor — 'well, we can decide later. For the next two days, at any rate, our direction would be the same practically in either case. If you have finished breakfast let's go and get under way.'

Upstairs I found our vessel surrounded by white and grey seagulls who flashed and circled about in the sunny morning air, looking for food scraps thrown out by the ships into the harbour.

By about half past seven we had the anchor up and the sails set to a nice steady breeze, and this time we got out into the open sea without bumping into a single thing. We met the Penzance fishing fleet coming in from the night's fishing, and very trim and neat they looked, in a line like soldiers, with their red-brown sails all leaning over the same way and the white water dancing before their bows.

For the next three or four days everything

went smoothly. We divided the twenty-four hours of the day into three spells, and we took it in turns to sleep our eight hours and be awake sixteen. So the ship was well looked after, with two of us always on duty.

Besides that, Polynesia, who was an older sailor than any of us, and really knew a lot about running ships, seemed to be always awake — except when she took her couple of winks in the sun, standing on one leg beside the wheel. You may be sure that no one ever got a chance to stay abed more than his eight hours while Polynesia was around. She used to watch the ship's clock, and if you overslept a half minute, she would come down to the cabin and peck you gently on the nose till you got up.

I very soon grew to be quite fond of our funny friend Bumpo, with his grand way of speaking and his enormous feet which some-one was always stepping on or falling over. Although he was much older than I was and had been to college, he never tried to lord it over me. He seemed to be forever smiling and kept all of us in good humour. It wasn't long before I began to see the Doctor's good sense in bringing him — in spite of the fact that he knew nothing whatever about sailing or travel.

On the morning of the fifth day out, just as I was taking the wheel over from the Doctor, Bumpo appeared and said, 'The salt beef is nearly all gone, sir.'

'The salt beef!' cried the Doctor. 'Why, we brought a hundred and twenty pounds with us. We couldn't have eaten that in five days. What can have become of it?'

'I don't know, sir, I'm sure. Every time I go down to the stores I find another hunk missing. If it is rats that are eating it, then they are certainly colossal rodents.'

Polynesia, who was walking up and down a stayrope taking her morning exercise, put in, 'We must search the hold. If this is allowed to go on, we will all be starving before a week is out. Come downstairs with me, Tommy, and we will look into this matter.'

So we went downstairs into the storeroom and Polynesia told us to keep quite still and listen. This we did. And presently we heard from a dark corner of the hold the distinct sound of someone snoring.

'Ah, I thought so,' said Polynesia. 'It's a man – and a big one. Climb in there, both of you, and haul him out. It sounds as though he were behind that barrel. Gosh! We seem to have brought half of Puddleby with us. Haul him out.'

So Bumpo and I lit a lantern and climbed over the stores. And there behind the barrel, sure enough, we found an enormous bearded man fast asleep with a well-fed look on his face. We woke him up.

'Washamarrer?' he said sleepily.

It was Ben Butcher, the able seaman.

Polynesia spluttered like an angry firecracker.

'This is the last straw,' said she. 'The one man in the world we least wanted. Shiver my timbers, what cheek!'

'Would it not be advisable,' suggested Bumpo, 'while the varlet is still sleepy, to strike him on the head with some heavy object and push him through a porthole into the sea?'

'No. We'd get into trouble,' said Polynesia. 'Besides, there never was a porthole big enough to push that man through. Bring him upstairs to the Doctor.'

So we led the man to the wheel, where he respectfully touched his cap to the Doctor.

'Another stowaway, sir,' said Bumpo smartly.

I thought the poor Doctor would have a fit.

'Good morning, Captain,' said the man. 'Ben Butcher, able seaman, at your service. I knew you'd need me, so I took the liberty of stowing away – much against my conscience. But I just couldn't bear to see you poor landsmen set out on this voyage without a single real seaman to help you. You'd never have got home alive if I hadn't come. Why look at your mainsail, sir – all loose at the throat. First gust of wind come along, and away goes your canvas overboard. Well, it's all right now I'm here. We'll soon get things in shipshape.'

'No, it isn't all right,' said the Doctor, 'it's all wrong. And I'm not at all glad to see you. I told you in Puddleby I didn't want you. You had no right to come.'

'But, Captain,' said the able seaman, 'you can't sail this ship without me. You don't understand navigation. Why, look at the compass now: you've let her swing a point and a half off her course. It's madness for you to try to do this trip alone – if you'll pardon my saying so, sir. Why . . . why, you'll lose the ship!'

'Look here,' said the Doctor, a sudden stern look coming into his eyes, 'losing a ship is nothing to me. I've lost ships before and it doesn't bother me in the least. When I set out to go to a place, I get there. Do you understand? I may know nothing whatever about sailing and navigation, but I get there just the same. Now you may be the best seaman in the world, but on *this* ship you're just a plain ordinary nuisance — very plain and very ordinary. And I am now going to call at the nearest port and put you ashore.'

'Yes, and think yourself lucky,' Polynesia put in, 'that you are not locked up for stowing away and eating all our salt beef.'

'I don't know what the mischief we're going to do now,' I heard her whisper to Bumpo. 'We've no money to buy any more, and that salt beef was the most important part of the stores.'

'Would it not be good political economy,' Bumpo whispered back, 'if we salted the able seaman and ate him instead? I should judge that he would weigh more than a hundred and twenty pounds.'

'Don't be silly,' snapped Polynesia. 'Those things are not done. — Still,' she murmured after a moment's thought, 'it's an awfully bright idea. I don't suppose anybody saw him come on to the ship. . . . Oh, but heavens! We haven't got enough salt. Besides, he'd be sure to taste of tobacco.'

Chapter Five
POLYNESIA HAS A PLAN

THEN the Doctor told me to take the wheel while he made a little calculation with his map and worked out what new course we should take.

'I shall have to run for the Capa Blancas after all,' he told me when the seaman's back was turned. 'Dreadful nuisance! But I'd sooner swim back to Puddleby than have to listen to that fellow's talk all the way to Brazil.'

Indeed he was a terrible person, this Ben Butcher. You'd think that anyone after being told he wasn't wanted would have had the decency to keep quiet. But not Ben Butcher. He kept going round the deck pointing out all the things we had wrong. According to him, there wasn't a thing right on the whole ship. The anchor was hitched up wrong; the hatches weren't fastened down properly; the sails were put on back to front; all our knots were the wrong kind of knots.

At last the Doctor told him to stop talking and go downstairs. He refused – said he wasn't going to be sunk by landlubbers while he was still able to stay on deck.

This made us feel a little uneasy. He was such an enormous man there was no knowing what he might do if he got really obstreperous.

Bumpo and I were talking about this downstairs in the dining saloon when Polynesia, Jip, and Chee-Chee came and joined us. And, as usual, Polynesia had a plan.

'Listen,' she said, 'I am certain this Ben Butcher is a smuggler and a bad man. I am a very good judge of seamen, remember, and I don't like the cut of this man's jib. I—'

'Do you really think,' I interrupted, 'that it *is* safe for the Doctor to cross the Atlantic without any regular seamen on his ship?'

You see it had upset me quite a good deal to find that all the things we had been doing were wrong; and I was beginning to wonder

what might happen if we ran into a storm —
particularly as Miranda had said the
weather would be good only for a certain
time, and we seemed to be having so many
delays. But Polynesia merely tossed her
head scornfully.

'Oh, bless you, my boy,' said she, 'you're
always safe with John Dolittle. Remember
that. Don't take any notice of that stupid old
salt. Of course it is perfectly true the Doctor
does do everything wrong. But with him it
doesn't matter. Mark my words, if you travel
with John Dolittle you always get there, as
you heard him say. I've been with him lots of
times and I know. Sometimes the ship is up-
side down when you get there, and sometimes it's right way up. But you get there just
the same. And then of course there's another
thing about the Doctor,' she added thoughtfully, 'he always has extraordinary good
luck. He may have his troubles, but with him
things seem to have a habit of turning out all
right in the end. I remember once when we
were going through the Straits of Magellan
the wind was so strong—'

'But what are we going to do about Ben
Butcher?' Jip put in. 'You had some plan,
Polynesia, hadn't you?'

'Yes. What I'm afraid of is that he may hit the Doctor on the head when he's not looking and make himself captain of *The Curlew*. Bad sailors do that sometimes. Then they run the ship their own way and take it where they want. That's what you call a mutiny.'

'Yes,' said Jip, 'and we ought to do something pretty quick. We can't reach the Capa Blancas before the day after tomorrow, at best. I don't like to leave the Doctor alone with him for a minute. He smells like a very bad man to me.'

'Well, I've got it all worked out,' said Polynesia. 'Listen, is there a key in that door?'

We looked outside the dining room and found that there was.

'All right,' said Polynesia. 'Now Bumpo lays the table for lunch and we all go and hide. Then at twelve o'clock Bumpo rings the dinner bell down here. As soon as Ben hears it he'll come down expecting more salt beef. Bumpo must hide behind the door outside. The moment that Ben is seated at the dining table Bumpo slams the door and locks it. Then we've got him. See?'

'How stratagenious!' Bumpo chuckled. 'As Cicero said, *parrots cum parishioners facilime congregation.* I'll lay the table at once.'

'Yes and take that Worcestershire sauce off the dresser with you when you go out,' said Polynesia. 'Don't leave any loose eatables around. That fellow has had enough to last any man for three days. Besides, he won't be so inclined to start a fight when we put him ashore at the Capa Blancas if we thin him down a bit before we let him out.'

So we all went and hid ourselves in the passage where we could watch what happened. And presently Bumpo came to the foot of the stairs and rang the dinner bell like mad. Then he hopped behind the dining room door and we all kept still and listened.

Almost immediately, *thump, thump, thump,* down the stairs tramped Ben Butcher, the able seaman. He walked into the dining saloon, sat himself down at the head of the table in the Doctor's place, tucked a napkin under his fat chin, and heaved a sigh of expectation.

Then, *bang!* Bumpo slammed the door and locked it.

'That settles *him* for a while,' said Polynesia coming out from her hiding place.

'Now let him teach navigation to the sideboard. Gosh, the cheek of the man! I've forgotten more about the sea than that lumbering lout will ever know. Let's go upstairs and tell the Doctor. Bumpo you will have to serve the meals in the cabin for the next couple of days.'

And bursting into a rollicking Norwegian sea song, she climbed up to my shoulder and we went on deck.

Chapter Six
THE BED MAKER
OF MONTEVERDE

WE remained three days in the Capa Blanca Islands.

There were two reasons why we stayed there so long when we were really in such a hurry to get away. One was the shortage in our provisions caused by the able seaman's enormous appetite. When we came to go over the stores and make a list, we found that he had eaten a whole lot of other things beside the beef. And having no money, we were sorely puzzled how to buy more. The Doctor went through his trunk to see if there was anything he could sell. But the only thing he could find was an old watch with the hands broken and the back dented in, and we decided this would not bring in enough money to buy much more than a

pound of tea. Bumpo suggested that he sing
comic songs in the streets which he had
learned in Jolliginki. But the Doctor said he
did not think that the islanders would pay
for music when they could make their own.

The other thing that kept us was the
bullfight. In these islands, which belonged
to Spain, they had bullfights every Sunday.
It was on a Friday that we arrived there,
and after we had got rid of the able seaman
we took a walk through the town.

It was a very funny little town, quite different from any that I had ever seen. The
streets were all twisty and winding and so
narrow that a wagon could only just pass
along them. The houses overhung at the top
and came so close together that people in the
attics could lean out of the windows and
shake hands with their neighbours on the
opposite side of the street. The Doctor told
us the town was very, very old. It was called
Monteverde.

As we had no money of course we did not
go to a hotel or anything like that. But on
the second evening when we were passing
by a bed maker's shop we noticed several
beds, which the man had made, standing on
the pavement outside. The Doctor started

chatting in Spanish to the bed maker, who was sitting at his door whistling to a parrot in a cage. The Doctor and the bed maker got very friendly talking about birds and things. And as it grew near to supper-time the man asked us to stop and sup with him.

This of course we were very glad to do. And after the meal was over (very nice dishes they were, mostly cooked in olive oil – I particularly liked the fried bananas) we sat outside on the pavement again and went on talking far into the night.

At last when we got up to go back to our ship, this very nice shopkeeper wouldn't hear of our going away on any account. He said the streets down by the harbour were very badly lit and there was no moon. We would surely get lost. He invited us to spend the night with him and go back to our ship in the morning.

Well, we finally agreed; and as our good friend had no spare bedrooms, the three of us, the Doctor, Bumpo and I, slept on the beds set out for sale on the pavement before the shop. The night was so hot we needed no coverings. It was great fun to fall asleep out-of-doors like this, watching the people walking to and fro and the gay life of the streets.

'The Doctor started chatting in Spanish
to the bed maker'

It seemed to me that Spanish people never went to bed at all. Late as it was, all the little restaurants and cafés around us were wide open, with customers drinking coffee and chatting merrily at the small tables outside. The sound of a guitar strumming softly in the distance mingled with the clatter of chinaware and the babble of voices.

Somehow it made me think of my mother and father far away in Puddleby, with their regular habits, the evening practice on the flute and the rest – doing the same thing every day. I felt sort of sorry for them, in a way, because they missed the fun of this travelling life, where we were doing something new all the time – even sleeping differently. But I suppose if they had been invited to go to bed on a pavement in front of a shop they wouldn't have cared for the idea at all. It is funny how some people are.

Chapter Seven
THE DOCTOR'S WAGER

NEXT morning we were awakened by a great racket. There was a procession coming down the street, a number of men in very gay clothes followed by a large crowd of admiring ladies and cheering children. I asked the Doctor who they were.

'They are the bullfighters,' he said. 'There is to be a bullfight tomorrow.'

'What is a bullfight?' I asked

To my great surprise, the Doctor got red in the face with anger. It reminded me of the time when he had spoken of the lions and tigers in his private zoo.

'A bullfight is a stupid, cruel, disgusting business,' said he. 'These Spanish people are most lovable and hospitable folk. How they can enjoy these wretched bullfights is a thing I could never understand.'

Then the Doctor went on to explain to me how a bull was first made very angry by teasing and then allowed to run into a circus where men came out with red cloaks, waved them at him, and ran away. Next the bull was allowed to tire himself out by tossing and killing a lot of poor old broken-down horses who couldn't defend themselves. Then, when the bull was thoroughly out of breath and wearied by this, a man came out with a sword and killed the bull.

'Every Sunday,' said the Doctor, 'in almost every big town in Spain there are six bulls killed like that and as many horses.'

'But aren't the men ever killed by the bull?' I asked.

'Unfortunately very seldom,' said he. 'A bull is not nearly as dangerous as he looks, even when he's angry, if only you are quick on your feet and don't lose your head. These bullfighters are very clever and nimble. And the people, especially the Spanish ladies, think no end of them. A famous bullfighter (or matador, as they call them) is a more important man in Spain than a king – here comes another crowd of them round the corner, look. See the girls throwing kisses to them. Ridiculous business!'

At that moment our friend the bed maker came out to see the procession go past. And while he was wishing us a good morning and inquiring how we slept, a friend of his walked up and joined us. The bed maker introduced this friend to us as Don Enrique Cardenas.

Don Enrique, when he heard where we were from, spoke to us in English. He appeared to be a well-educated, gentlemanly sort of person.

'And you go to see the bullfight tomorrow, yes?' he asked the Doctor pleasantly.

'Certainly not,' said John Dolittle firmly. 'I don't like bullfights — cruel, cowardly shows.'

Don Enrique nearly exploded. I never saw a man get so excited. He told the Doctor that he didn't know what he was talking about. He said bullfighting was a noble sport and that the matadors were the bravest men in the world.

'Oh, rubbish!' said the Doctor. 'You never give the poor bull a chance. It is only when he is all tired and dazed that your precious matadors dare to try and kill him.'

I thought the Spaniard was going to strike the Doctor, he got so angry. While he was still spluttering to find words, the bed maker came between them and took the Doctor aside. He explained to John Dolittle in a whisper that this Don Enrique Cardenas was a very important person, that he it was who supplied the bulls – a special, strong black kind – from his own farm for all the bullfights in the Capa Blancas. He was a very rich man, the bed maker said, a most important personage. He mustn't be allowed to take offence on any account.

I watched the Doctor's face as the bed maker finished, and I saw a flash of boyish mischief come into his eyes as though an idea had struck him. He turned to the angry Spaniard.

'Don Enrique,' he said, 'you tell me your bullfighters are very brave men and skilful. It seems I have offended you by saying that bullfighting is a poor sport. What is the name of the best matador for tomorrow's show?'

'Pepito de Malaga,' said Don Enrique, 'one of the greatest names, one of the bravest men, in all Spain.'

'Very well,' said the Doctor, 'I have a

proposal to make to you. I have never fought
a bull in my life. Now supposing I were to go
into the ring tomorrow with Pepito de
Malaga and any other matadors you choose,
and if I can do more tricks with a bull than
they can, would you promise to do something for me?'

Don Enrique threw back his head and
laughed.

'Man,' he said, 'you must be mad! You
would be killed at once. One has to be
trained for years to become a proper bullfighter.'

'Supposing I were willing to take the risk
of that . . . you are not afraid, I take it, to
accept my offer?'

The Spaniard frowned.

'Afraid!' he cried. 'Sir, if you can beat
Pepito de Malaga in the bullring I'll promise
you anything it is possible for me to grant.'

'Very good,' said the Doctor. 'Now I understand that you are quite a powerful man in
these islands. If you wished to stop all
bullfighting here after tomorrow, you could
do it, couldn't you?'

'Yes,' said Don Enrique proudly, 'I could.'

'Well, that is what I ask of you – if I win
my wager,' said John Dolittle. 'If I can do

more with angry bulls than can Pepito de Malaga, you are to promise me that there shall never be another bullfight in the Capa Blancas so long as you are alive to stop it. Is it a bargain?'

The Spaniard held out his hand.

'It is a bargain,' he said. 'I promise. But I must warn you that you are merely throwing your life away, for you will certainly be killed. However, that is no more than you deserve for saying that bullfighting is an unworthy sport. I will meet you here tomorrow morning if you should wish to arrange any particulars. Good day, sir.'

As the Spaniard turned and walked into the shop with the bed maker, Polynesia, who had been listening as usual, flew up on to my shoulder and whispered in my ear, 'I have a plan. Get hold of Bumpo and come some place where the Doctor can't hear us. I want to talk to you.'

I nudged Bumpo's elbow and we crossed the street and pretended to look into a jeweller's window, while the Doctor sat down upon his bed to lace up his boots, the only part of his clothing he had taken off for the night.

'Listen,' said Polynesia, 'I've been breaking

my head trying to think up some way we can get money to buy those stores with, and at last I've got it.'

'The money?' said Bumpo.

'No, the idea – to make the money with. Listen, the Doctor is simply bound to win this game tomorrow, sure as you're alive. Now all we have to do is to make a side bet with these Spaniards and the trick's done.'

'What's a side bet?' I asked.

'Oh, I know what that is,' said Bumpo proudly. 'We used to have lots of them at Oxford when boat-racing was on. I go to Don Enrique and say, "I bet you a hundred pounds the Doctor wins." Then if he does win, Don Enrique pays me a hundred pounds; and if he doesn't, I have to pay Don Enrique.'

'That's the idea,' said Polynesia. 'Only don't say a hundred pounds – say two thousand five hundred pesetas. Now, come and find old Don Ricky-ticky and try to look rich.'

So we crossed the street again and slipped into the bed maker's shop while the Doctor was still busy with his boots.

'Don Enrique,' said Bumpo, 'allow me to introduce myself. I am the Crown Prince of

Jolliginki. Would you care to have a small bet with me on tomorrow's bullfight?'

Don Enrique bowed.

'Why certainly,' he said, 'I shall be delighted. But I must warn you that you are bound to lose. How much?'

'Oh a mere truffle,' said Bumpo – 'just for the fun of the thing, you know. What do you say to three thousand pesetas?'

'I agree,' said the Spaniard, bowing once more. 'I will meet you after the bullfight tomorrow.'

'So that's all right,' said Polynesia as we came out to join the Doctor. 'I feel as though quite a load had been taken off my mind.'

Chapter Eight
THE GREAT BULLFIGHT

THE next day was a great day in Monteverde. All the streets were hung with flags, and everywhere gaily dressed crowds were to be seen flocking towards the bull-ring, as the big circus was called where the fights took place.

The news of the Doctor's challenge had gone round the town and, it seemed, had caused much amusement to the islanders. The very idea of a mere foreigner daring to match himself against the great Pepito de Malaga! . . . Serve him right if he got killed!

The Doctor had borrowed a bullfighter's suit from Don Enrique; and very gay and wonderful he looked in it, though Bumpo and I had hard work getting the waistcoat to close in front and, even then, the buttons kept bursting off it in all directions.

When we set out from the harbour to walk to the bull ring, crowds of small boys ran after us making fun of the Doctor's fatness, calling out, *'Juan Hagapoco, el gruesto matador!'* which is Spanish for 'John Dolittle, the fat bullfighter.'

As soon as we arrived the Doctor said he would like to take a look at the bulls before the fight began, and we were at once led to the bull pen where, behind a high railing, six enormous black bulls were tramping round wildly.

In a few hurried words and signs the Doctor told the bulls what he was going to do and gave them careful instructions for their part of the show. The poor creatures were tremendously glad when they heard that there was a chance of bullfighting being stopped, and they promised to do exactly as they were told.

Of course the man who took us in there didn't understand what we were doing. He merely thought the fat Englishman was crazy when he saw the doctor making signs and talking in ox tongue.

From there the Doctor went to the

matadors' dressing rooms while Bumpo and I with Polynesia made our way into the bull-ring and took our seats in the great open-air theatre.

It was a very gay sight. Thousands of ladies and gentlemen were there, all dressed in their smartest clothes, and everybody seemed very happy and cheerful.

Right at the beginning Don Enrique got up and explained to the people that the first item on the programme was to be a match between the English Doctor and Pepito de Malaga. He told them what he had promised if the Doctor should win. But the people did not seem to think there was much chance of that. A roar of laughter went up at the very mention of such a thing.

When Pepito came into the ring everybody cheered, the ladies blew kisses, and the men clapped and waved their hats.

Presently a large door on the other side of the ring was rolled back and in galloped one of the bulls; then the door was closed again. At once the matador became very much on the alert. He waved his red cloak and the bull rushed at him. Pepito stepped nimbly aside and the people cheered again.

This game was repeated several times.

But I noticed that whenever Pepito got into a tight place and seemed to be in real danger from the bull, an assistant of his, who always hung around somewhere near, drew the bull's attention upon himself by waving another red cloak. Then the bull would chase the assistant and Pepito was left in safety. Most often, as soon as he had drawn the bull off, this assistant ran for the high fence and vaulted out of the ring to save himself. They evidently had it all arranged, these matadors, and it didn't seem to me that they were in any very great danger from the poor clumsy bull so long as they didn't slip and fall.

After about ten minutes of this kind of thing the small door into the matadors' dressing room opened and the Doctor strolled into the ring. As soon as his fat figure, dressed in sky-blue velvet, appeared, the crowd rocked in their seats with laughter.

Juan Hagapoco, as they had called him, walked out into the centre of the ring and bowed ceremoniously to the ladies in the boxes. Then he bowed to the bull. Then he bowed to Pepito. While he was bowing to Pepito's assistant the bull started to rush at him from behind.

'Look out! Look out! The bull! You will be killed!' yelled the crowd.

But the Doctor calmly finished his bow. Then turning round he folded his arms, fixed the onrushing bull with his eye and frowned a terrible frown.

Presently a curious thing happened: the bull's speed got slower and slower. It almost looked as though he were afraid of that frown. Soon he stopped altogether. The Doctor shook his finger at him. He began to tremble. At last, tucking his tail between his legs, the bull turned round and ran away.

The crowd gasped. The Doctor ran after him. Round and round the ring they went, both of them puffing and blowing like grampuses. Excited whispers began to break out among the people. This was something new in bullfighting, to have the bull running away from the man instead of the man away from the bull. At last in the tenth lap, with a final burst of speed, Juan Hagapoco, the English matador, caught the poor bull by the tail.

Then leading the now timid creature into the middle of the ring, the Doctor made him do all manner of tricks: standing on the hind

'Did acrobatics on the beast's horns'

legs, standing on the front legs, dancing, hopping, rolling over. He finished up by making the bull kneel down; then he got on to his back and did handsprings and other acrobatics on the beast's horns.

Pepito and his assistant had their noses sadly out of joint. The crowd had forgotten them entirely. They were standing together by the fence not far from where I sat, muttering to one another and slowly growing green with jealousy.

Finally the Doctor turned towards Don Enrique's seat and bowing said in a loud voice, 'This bull is no good any more. He's terrified and out of breath. Take him away, please.'

'Does the caballero wish for a fresh bull?' asked Don Enrique.

'No,' said the Doctor, 'I want five fresh bulls. And I would like them all in the ring at once, please.'

At this, a cry of horror burst from the people. They had been used to seeing matadors escaping from one bull at a time but *five*! . . . That must mean certain death.

Pepito sprang forward and called to Don Enrique not to allow it, saying it was against all the rules of bullfighting. ('Ha!'

Polynesia chuckled into my ear. 'It's like the Doctor's navigation: he breaks all the rules, but he gets there. If they'll only let him, he'll give them the best show for their money they ever saw.') A great argument began. Half the people seemed to be on Pepito's side and half on the Doctor's side. At last the Doctor turned to Pepito and made another very grand bow which burst the last button off his waistcoat.

'Well, of course if the caballero is afraid—' he began with a bland smile.

'Afraid!' screamed Pepito. 'I am afraid of nothing on earth. I am the greatest matador in Spain. With this right hand I have killed nine hundred and fifty-seven bulls.'

'All right then,' said the Doctor, 'let us see if you can kill five more. Let the bulls in!' he shouted. 'Pepito de Malaga is not afraid.'

A dreadful silence hung over the great theatre as the heavy door in the bull pen was rolled back. Then with a roar the five big bulls bounded into the ring.

'Look fierce,' I heard the Doctor call to them in cattle language. 'Don't scatter. Keep close. Get ready for a rush. Take Pepito, the one in purple, first. But for heaven's sake don't kill him. Just chase him out of the ring. Now then, all together, go for him!'

The bulls put down their heads and all in line, like a squadron of cavalry, charged across the ring straight for poor Pepito.

For one moment the Spaniard tried his hardest to look brave. But the sight of the five pairs of horns coming at him at full gallop was too much. He turned white to the lips, ran for the fence, vaulted it, and disappeared.

'Now the other one,' the Doctor hissed. And in two seconds the gallant assistant was nowhere to be seen. Juan Hagapoco, the fat matador, was left alone in the ring with five rampaging bulls.

The rest of the show was really well worth seeing. First, all five bulls went raging round the ring, butting at the fence with their horns, pawing up the sand, hunting for something to kill. Then each one in turn would pretend to catch sight of the Doctor for the first time and, giving a bellow of rage, would lower his wicked-looking horns and shoot like an arrow across the ring as though he meant to toss him to the sky.

It was really frightfully exciting. And even I, who knew it was all arranged beforehand, held my breath in terror for the Doctor's life when I saw how near they came to sticking him. But just at the last moment, when the horns' points were two inches from the sky-blue waistcoat, the Doctor would spring nimbly to one side and the great brutes would go thundering harmlessly by, missing him by no more than a hair.

Then all five of them went for him together, completely surrounding him, slashing at him with their horns and bellowing with fury. How he escaped alive I don't know. For several minutes his round figure could hardly be seen at all in that scrimmage of tossing heads, stamping hoofs, and waving tails. It was, as Polynesia had prophesied, the greatest bullfight ever seen.

One woman in the crowd got quite hysterical and screamed up to Don Enrique, 'Stop the fight! Stop the fight! He is too brave a man to be killed. This is the most wonderful matador in the world. Let him live! Stop the fight!'

But presently the Doctor was seen to break loose from the mob of animals that surrounded him. Then catching each of them by the horns, one after another, he would give their heads a sudden twist and throw them down flat on the sand. The great fellows acted their parts extremely well. I have never seen trained animals in a circus do better. They lay there panting on the ground where the Doctor threw them as if they were exhausted and completely beaten.

Then with a final bow to the ladies John Dolittle took a cigar from his pocket, lit it, and strolled out of the ring.

Chapter Nine
WE DEPART IN A HURRY

AS soon as the door closed behind the Doctor the most tremendous noise I have ever heard broke loose. Some of the men appeared to be angry (friends of Pepito's, I suppose), but the ladies called and called to have the Doctor come back into the ring.

When at length he did so, the women seemed to go entirely mad over him. They blew kisses to him. They called him a darling. Then they started taking off their flowers, their rings, their necklaces, and their brooches and threw them down at his feet. You never saw anything like it – a perfect shower of jewellery and roses.

But the Doctor just smiled up at them, bowed once more, and backed out.

'Now, Bumpo,' said Polynesia, 'this is where you go down and gather up all those trinkets and we'll sell 'em. That's what the big matadors do: leave the jewellery on the ground and their assistants collect it for them. We might as well lay in a good supply of money while we've got the chance – you never know when you may need it when you're travelling with the Doctor. Never mind the roses – you can leave them – but don't leave any rings. And when you've finished go and get your three thousand pesetas out of Don Ricky-ticky. Tommy and I will meet you outside and we'll pawn the gewgaws at that shop opposite the bed maker's. Run along – and not a word to the Doctor, remember.'

Outside the Bull-ring we found the crowd still in a great state of excitement. Violent arguments were going on everywhere. Bumpo joined us with his pockets bulging in all directions, and we made our way slowly through the dense crowd to that side of the building where the matadors' dressing room was. The Doctor was waiting at the door for us.

'Good work, Doctor!' said Polynesia, flying on to his shoulder. 'Great work! But listen,

I smell danger. I think you had better get back to the ship now as quickly and quietly as you can. Put your overcoat on over that giddy suit. I don't like the looks of this crowd. More than half of them are furious because you've won. Don Ricky-ticky must now stop the bullfighting – and you know how they love it. What I'm afraid of is that some of these matadors who are just mad with jealousy may start some dirty work. I think this would be a good time for us to get away.'

'I dare say you're right, Polynesia,' said the Doctor – 'you usually are. The crowd does seem to be a bit restless. I'll slip down to the ship alone so I shan't be so noticeable, and I'll wait for you there. You come by some different way. But don't be long about it. Hurry!'

As soon as the Doctor had departed Bumpo sought out Don Enrique and said, 'Honourable Sir, you owe me three thousand pesetas.'

Without a word, but looking cross-eyed with annoyance, Don Enrique paid his bet.

We next set out to buy the provisions, and on the way we hired a cab and took it along with us.

Not very far away we found a big grocer's shop which seemed to sell everything to eat. We went in and bought the finest lot of food you ever saw in your life.

As a matter of fact, Polynesia had been right about the danger we were in. The news of our victory must have spread like lightning through the whole town. For as we came out of the shop and loaded the cab up with our stores, we saw various little knots of angry men hunting around the streets, waving sticks and shouting, 'The Englishmen! Where are those accursed Englishmen who stopped the bullfighting? Hang them from a lamp-post! Throw them in the sea! The Englishmen! . . . We want the Englishmen!'

After that we didn't waste any time, you may be sure. Bumpo grabbed the Spanish cab-driver and explained to him in signs that if he didn't drive down to the harbour as fast as he knew how and keep his mouth shut the whole way, he would choke the life out of him. Then he jumped into the cab on top of the food, slammed the door, pulled down the blinds, and away we went.

'We won't get a chance to pawn the jewellery now,' said Polynesia, as we bumped over the cobbly streets. 'But never mind – it may come in handy later on. And, anyway, we've got two thousand five hundred pesetas left out of the bet. Don't give the cabby more than two pesetas fifty, Bumpo. That's the right fare, I know.'

Well, we reached the harbour all right and we were mighty glad to find the Doctor had sent Chee-Chee back with the rowing boat to wait for us at the landing wall.

Unfortunately, while we were in the middle of loading the supplies from the cab into the boat, the angry mob arrived upon the wharf and made a rush for us. Bumpo snatched up a big beam of wood that lay near and swung it round and round his head, letting out dreadful African battle yells the while. This kept the crowd off while Chee-Chee and I hustled the last of the stores into the boat and clambered in ourselves. Bumpo threw his beam of wood into the thick of the Spaniards and leapt in after us. Then we pushed off and rowed like mad for *The Curlew*.

The mob upon the wall howled with rage, shook their fists, and hurled stones and all manner of things after us. Poor old Bumpo got hit on the head with a bottle. But as he had a very strong head it only raised a small bump, while the bottle smashed into a thousand pieces.

When he reached the ship's side the Doctor had the anchor drawn up and the sails set and everything in readiness to get away. Looking back we saw boats coming out from the harbour wall after us, filled with angry, shouting men. So we didn't bother to unload our rowing boat but just tied it on to the ship's stern with a rope and jumped aboard.

It took only a moment more to swing *The Curlew* round into the wind, and soon we were speeding out of the harbour on our way to Brazil.

'Ha!' sighed Polynesia, as we all flopped down on the deck to take a rest and get our breath. 'That wasn't a bad adventure – quite reminds me of my old seafaring days when I sailed with the smugglers. Golly, that was the life! Never mind your head, Bumpo. It will be all right when the Doctor puts a little arnica on it. Think what we got out of the scrap: a boatload of ship's stores, pockets full of jewellery, and thousands of pesetas. Not bad, you know – not bad.'

PART IV

Chapter One
SHELLFISH LANGUAGES AGAIN

MIRANDA, the purple bird of paradise, had prophesied rightly when she had foretold a good spell of weather. For three weeks the good ship *Curlew* ploughed her way through smiling seas before a steady powerful wind.

We did not pass many ships. When we did see one, the Doctor would get out his telescope and we would all take a look at it. Sometimes he would signal to it, asking for news by hauling up little coloured flags upon the mast; and the ship would signal back to us in the same way. The meaning of all the signals was printed in a book that the Doctor kept in the cabin. He told me it was the language of the sea and that all ships could understand it, whether they be English, Dutch, or French.

Our greatest happening during those first weeks was passing an iceberg. When the sun shone on it, it burst into a hundred colours, sparkling like a jewelled palace in a fairy story. Through the telescope we saw a mother polar bear with a cub sitting on it, watching us. The Doctor recognized her as one of the bears who had spoken to him when he was discovering the North Pole. So he sailed the ship up close and offered to take her and her baby on to *The Curlew* if she wished it. But she only shook her head, thanking him. She said it would be far too hot for the cub on the deck of our ship, with no ice to keep his feet cool. It had been indeed a very hot day, but the nearness of that great mountain of ice made us all turn up our coat collars and shiver with the cold.

One afternoon we saw, floating around us, great quantities of stuff that looked like dead grass. The Doctor told me this was gulfweed. A little further on it became so thick that it covered all the water as far as the eye could reach. It made *The Curlew* look as though she were moving across a meadow instead of sailing the Atlantic.

Crawling about upon this weed, many crabs were to be seen. And the sight of them reminded the Doctor of his dream of learning the language of the shellfish. He fished several of these crabs up with a net and put them in his listening-tank to see if he could understand them. Among the crabs he also caught a strange-looking, chubby little fish which he told me was called a silver fidgit.

After he had listened to the crabs for a while with no success, he put the fidgit into the tank and began to listen to that. I had to leave him at this moment to go and attend to some duties on the deck. But presently I heard him below shouting for me to come down again.

'Stubbins,' he cried as soon as he saw me, 'a most extraordinary thing . . . quite unbelievable . . . I'm not sure whether I'm dreaming . . . can't believe my own senses. I–I–I—'

'Why, Doctor,' I said, 'what is it? What's the matter?'

'The fidgit,' he whispered, pointing with a trembling finger to the listening-tank in which the little round fish was still swimming quietly, 'he talks English! And . . . and . . . and *he whistles tunes* – English tunes!'

'Talks English!' I cried. 'Whistles! Why, it's impossible.'

'It's a fact,' said the Doctor. 'It's only a few words, scattered, with no particular sense to them – all mixed up with his own language, which I can't make out yet. But they're English words, unless there's something very wrong with my hearing. And the tune he whistles, it's as plain as anything – always the same tune. Now you listen and tell me what you make of it. Tell me everything you hear. Don't miss a word.'

I went to the glass tank upon the table while the Doctor grabbed a notebook and a pencil. Undoing my collar I stood upon the empty packing case he had been using for a stand and put my ear right down under the water.

For some moments I detected nothing at all – except, with my dry ear, the heavy breathing of the Doctor as he waited, all stiff and anxious, for me to say something. At last from within the water, sounding like a child singing miles and miles away, I heard an unbelievably thin, small voice.

'Ah!' I said.

'What is it?' asked the Doctor in a hoarse, trembly whisper. 'What does he say?'

' "He talks English!" '

'I can't quite make it out,' I said. 'It's mostly in some strange fish language. Oh, but wait a minute! Yes, now I get it: "No smoking".... "My, here's a queer one!" "Popcorn and picture postcards here".... "This way out".... "Don't spit" – what funny things to say, Doctor! Oh, but wait! Now he's whistling the tune.'

'What tune is it?' gasped the Doctor.

'John Peel.'

'Aha!' cried the Doctor. 'That's what I made it out to be!' And he wrote furiously in his notebook.

I went on listening.

'This is most extraordinary!' the Doctor kept muttering to himself as his pencil went wiggling over the page. 'Most extraordinary, but frightfully thrilling! I wonder where he—'

'Here's some more,' I cried – 'some more English. *The big tank needs cleaning....*" That's all. Now he's talking fish talk again.'

'The big tank!' the Doctor murmured frowning in a puzzled kind of way. 'I wonder where on earth he learned—'

Then he bounded up out of his chair.

'I have it!' he yelled. 'This fish has escaped from an aquarium! Why, of course! Look at the kind of things he has learned: "Picture postcards" – they always sell them in aquariums; "Don't spit"; "No smoking"; "This way out" – the things the attendants say. And then, "My, here's a queer one!" That's the kind of thing that people exclaim when they look into the tanks. It all fits. There's no doubt about it, Stubbins: we have here a fish who has escaped from captivity. And it's quite possible now – not certain, by any means, but quite possible – that I may now, through him, be able to establish communication with the shellfish. This is a great piece of luck.'

Chapter Two
THE FIDGIT'S STORY

WELL, now that he was started once more upon his old hobby of the shellfish languages, there was no stopping the Doctor. He worked right through the night.

A little after midnight I fell asleep in a chair; about two in the morning Bumpo fell asleep at the wheel; and for five hours *The Curlew* was allowed to drift where she liked. But still John Dolittle worked on, trying his hardest to understand the fidgit's language, struggling to make the fidgit understand him.

When I woke up it was broad daylight again. The Doctor was still standing at the listening-tank, looking as tired as an owl and dreadfully wet. But on his face there was a proud and happy smile.

'Stubbins,' he said as soon as he saw me stir, 'I've done it. I've got the key to the fidgit's language. It's a frightfully difficult language – quite different from anything I ever heard. The only thing it reminds me of – slightly – is ancient Hebrew. It isn't shellfish, but it's a big step towards it. Now, the next thing, I want you to take a pencil and a fresh notebook and write down everything I say. The fidgit has promised to tell me the story of his life. I will translate it into English and you put it down in the book. Are you ready?'

Once more the Doctor lowered his ear beneath the level of the water; and as he began to speak, I started to write. And this is the story that the fidgit told us.

Thirteen Months in an Aquarium

'I was born in the Pacific Ocean, close to the coast of Chile. I was one of a family of two thousand five hundred and ten. Soon after our mother and father left us, we youngsters got scattered. The family was broken up by a herd of whales who chased us. I and my sister Clippa (she was my favourite sister) had a very narrow escape for our lives. As a rule, whales are not very hard to get away from if you are good at dodging – if you've only got a quick swerve. But this one that came after Clippa and myself was a very mean whale. Every time he lost us under a stone or something, he'd come back and hunt and hunt till he routed us out into the open again. I never saw such a nasty, persevering brute.

'Well, we shook him at last – though not before he had worried us for hundreds of miles northward, up the west coast of South America. But luck was against us that day. While we were resting and trying to get our breath, another family of fidgits came rushing by, shouting, "Come on! Swim for your lives! The dogfish are coming!"

'Now dogfish are particularly fond of fidgits. We are, you might say, their favourite food – and for that reason we always keep away from deep, muddy waters. What's more, dogfish are not easy to escape from; they are terribly fast and clever hunters. So up we had to jump and on again.

'After we had gone a few more hundred miles we looked back and saw that the dogfish were gaining on us. So we turned into a harbour. It happened to be one on the west coast of the United States. Here we guessed, and hoped, the dogfish would not be likely to follow us. As it happened, they didn't even see us turn in, but dashed on northward and we never saw them again. I hope they froze to death in the Arctic seas.

'But, as I said, luck was against us that day. While I and my sister were cruising gently around the ships anchored in the harbour looking for orange peels, a great delicacy with us – *swoop! bang!* – we were caught in a net.

'We struggled for all we were worth, but it was no use. The net was small-meshed and strongly made. Kicking and flipping we were hauled up the side of the ship and dumped down on the deck, high and dry in a blazing noonday sun.

'Here a couple of old men in whiskers and spectacles leaned over us, making strange sounds. Some codling had got caught in the net the same time as we were. These the old men threw back into the sea, but us they seemed to think very precious. They put us carefully into a large jar and after they had taken us on shore they went to a big house and changed us from the jar into glass boxes full of water. This house was on the edge of the harbour, and a small stream of seawater was made to flow through the glass tank so we could breathe properly. Of course we had never lived inside glass walls before, and at first we kept on trying to swim through them and got our noses awfully sore bumping the glass at full speed.

'Then followed weeks and weeks of weary idleness. They treated us well, so far as they knew how. The old fellows in spectacles came and looked at us proudly twice a day and saw that we had the proper food to eat, the right amount of light, and that the water was not too hot or too cold. But, oh, the dullness of that life! It seemed we were a kind of a show. At a certain hour every morning the big doors of the house were thrown open and everybody in the city who had nothing special to do came in and looked at us. There were other tanks filled with different kinds of fishes all round the walls of the big room. And the crowds would go from tank to tank, looking in at us through the glass – with their mouths open, like half-witted flounders. We got so sick of it that we used to open our mouths back at them, and this they seemed to think highly comical.

'One day my sister said to me, "Think you, Brother, that these strange creatures who have captured us can talk?"

' "Surely," I said. "Have you noticed that some talk with the lips only, some with the whole face, and yet others discourse with the hands? When they come quite close to the glass you can hear them. Listen!"

'At that moment a female, larger than the rest, pressed her nose up against the glass, pointed at me and said to her young behind her, "Oh look, here's a queer one!"

'And then we noticed that they nearly always said this when they looked in. And for a long time we thought that such was the whole extent of the language, this being a people of but few ideas. To help pass away the weary hours we learned it by heart, "Oh, look, here's a queer one!" But we never got to know what it meant. Other phrases, however, we did get the meaning of, and we even learned to read a little in people talk. Many big signs there were, set up upon the walls; and when we saw that the keepers stopped the people from spitting and smoking, pointed to these signs angrily and read them out loud, we knew then that these writings signified *No Smoking* and *Don't Spit*.

'Then in the evenings, after the crowd had gone, the same aged male, with one leg of wood, swept up the peanut shells with a broom every night. And while he was so doing he always whistled the same tune to himself. This melody we rather liked, and we learned that too by heart – thinking it was part of the language.

'Thus a whole year went by in this dismal place. Some days new fishes were brought in to the other tanks, and other days old fishes were taken out. At first we had hoped we would only be kept here for a while, and that after we had been looked at sufficiently we would be returned to freedom and the sea. But as month after month went by, and we were left undisturbed, our hearts grew heavy within our prison walls of glass and we spoke to one another less and less.

'One day, when the crowd was thickest in the big room, a woman with a red face fainted from the heat. I watched through the glass and saw that the rest of the people got highly excited – though to me it did not seem to be a matter of very great importance. They threw cold water on her and carried her out into the open air.

'This made me think mightily, and presently a great idea burst upon me.

' "Sister," I said, turning to poor Clippa who was sulking at the bottom of our prison trying to hide behind a stone from the stupid gaze of the children who thronged about our tank, "supposing that *we* pretended we were sick: do you think they would take us also from this stuffy house?"

' "Brother," said she wearily, "that they might do. But most likely they would throw us on a rubbish heap, where we would die in the hot sun."

' "But," said I, "why should they go abroad and seek a rubbish heap when the harbour is so close? While we were being brought here I saw men throwing their rubbish into the water. If they would only throw us also there, we could quickly reach the sea."

' "The sea!" murmured poor Clippa with a faraway look in her eyes (she had fine eyes, had my sister Clippa). "How like a dream it sounds — the sea! Oh, Brother, will we ever swim in it again, think you? Every night as I lie awake on the floor of this evil-smelling dungeon I hear its hearty voice ringing in my ears. How I have longed for it! Just to feel it once again, the nice, big, wholesome

homeliness of it all! To jump, just to jump
from the crest of an Atlantic wave, laughing
in the trade wind's spindrift, down into the
blue-green swirling trough! To chase the
shrimps on a summer evening, when the
sky is red and the light's all pink within the
foam! To lie on the top, in the doldrums'
noonday calm, and warm your tummy in the
tropic sun! To wander hand in hand once
more through the giant seaweed forests of
the Indian Ocean, seeking the delicious eggs
of the pop-pop! To play hide-and-seek among
the castles of the coral towns with their
pearl and jasper windows spangling the
floor of the Spanish Main! To picnic in the
anemone meadows, dim blue and lilac-grey,
that lie in the lowlands beyond the South
Sea Garden! To throw somersaults on the
springy sponge beds of the Mexican Gulf! To
poke about among the dead ships and see
what wonders and adventures lie inside!
And then, on winter nights when the north-
easter whips the water into froth, to swoop
down and down to get away from the cold,
down to where the water's warm and dark,
down and still down, till we spy the twinkle
of the fire eels far below where our friends
and cousins sit chatting round the council

grotto – chatting, Brother, over the news and gossip of *the sea*! . . . Oh—"

'And then she broke down completely, sniffling.

' "Stop it!" I said. "You make me homesick. Look here, let's pretend we're sick – or better still – let's pretend we're dead and see what happens. If they throw us on a rubbish heap and we fry in the sun, we'll not be much worse off than we are here in this smelly prison. What do you say? Will you risk it?"

' "I will," she said – "and gladly."

'So the next morning two fidgits were found by their keeper floating on the top of the water in their tank, stiff and dead. We gave a mighty good imitation of dead fish – although I say it myself. The keeper ran and got the old gentlemen with spectacles and whiskers. They threw up their hands in horror when they saw us. Lifting us carefully out of the water they laid us on wet cloths. That was the hardest part of all. If you're a fish and get taken out of the water you have to keep opening and shutting your mouth to breathe at all – and even that you can't keep up for long. And all this time we had to stay stiff as sticks and breathe silently through half-closed lips.

'Well, the old fellows poked us and felt us and pinched us till I thought they'd never be done. Then, when their backs were turned a moment, a wretched cat got up on the table and nearly ate us. Luckily the old men turned round in time and shooed her away. You may be sure though that we took a couple of good gulps of air while they weren't looking, and that was the only thing that saved us from choking. I wanted to whisper to Clippa to be brave and stick it out. But I couldn't even do that, because, as you know, most kinds of fish talk cannot be heard – not even a shout – unless you're under water.

'Then, just as we were about to give up and let on that we were alive, one of the old men shook his head sadly, lifted us up, and carried us out of the building.

' "Now for it!" I thought to myself. "We'll soon know our fate: liberty or the garbage can."

'Outside, to our unspeakable horror, he made straight for a large ash barrel, which stood against the wall on the other side of a yard. Most happily for us, however, while he was crossing this yard a very dirty man with a wagon and horses drove up and took the ash barrel away. I suppose it was his property.

'Then the old man looked around for some other place to throw us. He seemed about to cast us upon the ground. But he evidently thought that this would make the yard untidy and he desisted. The suspense was terrible. He moved outside the yard gate and my heart sank once more as I saw that he now intended to throw us in the gutter of the street. But (fortune was indeed with us that day), a large man in blue clothes and silver buttons stopped him in the nick of time. Evidently, from the way the large man lectured and waved a short, thick stick, it was against the rules of the town to throw dead fish in the streets.

'At last, to our unutterable joy, the old man turned and moved off with us towards the harbour. He walked so slowly, muttering to himself all the way and watching the man in blue out of the corner of his eye, that I wanted to bite his finger to make him hurry up. Both Clippa and I were actually at our last gasp.

'Finally he reached the sea wall and giving us one last sad look he dropped us into the waters of the harbour.

'Never had we realized anything like the thrill of that moment, as we felt the salt wetness close over our heads. With one flick of our tails we came to life again. The old man was so surprised that he fell right into the water, almost on top of us. From this he was rescued by a sailor with a boat hook; and the last we saw of him, the man in blue was dragging him away by the coat collar, lecturing him again. Apparently it was also against the rules of the town to throw dead fish into the harbour.

'But we? What time or thought had we for his troubles? *We were free!* In lightning leaps, in curving spurts, in crazy zigzags – whooping, shrieking with delight, we sped for home and the open sea!

'That is all of my story and I will now, as I promised last night, try to answer any questions you may ask about the sea, on condition that I am set at liberty as soon as you have done.'

The Doctor: Is there any part of the sea deeper than that known as the Nero Deep – I mean the one near the Island of Guam?
The Fidgit: Why, certainly. There's one much deeper than that near the mouth of

the Amazon River. But it's small and hard to find. We call it the Deep Hole. And there's another in the Antarctic Sea.

The Doctor: Can you talk any shellfish languages yourself?

The Fidgit: No, not a word. We regular fishes don't have anything to do with the shellfish. We consider them a low class.

The Doctor: But when you're near them, can you hear the sound they make talking – I mean without necessarily understanding what they say?

The Fidgit: Only with the very largest ones. Shellfish have such weak, small voices it is almost impossible for any but their own kind to hear them. But with the bigger ones it is different. They make a sad, booming noise, rather like an iron pipe being knocked with a stone – only not nearly so loud of course.

The Doctor: I am most anxious to get down to the bottom of the sea – to study many things. But we land animals, as you no doubt know, are unable to breathe under water. Have you any ideas that might help me?

The Fidgit: I think that for both your difficulties the best thing for you to do would be to try and get hold of the great glass sea snail.

The Doctor: Er – who, or what, is the great glass sea snail?

The Fidgit: He is an enormous saltwater snail, one of the winkle family, but as large as a big house. He talks quite loudly – when he speaks, but this is not often. He can go to any part of the ocean, at all depths because he doesn't have to be afraid of any creature in the sea. His shell is made of transparent mother-of-pearl so that you can see through it, but it's thick and strong. When he is out of his shell and he carries it empty on his back, there is room in it for a wagon and a pair of horses. He has been seen carrying his food in it when travelling.

The Doctor: I feel that that is just the creature I have been looking for. He could take me and my assistant inside his shell and we could explore the deepest depths in safety. Do you think you could get him for me?

The Fidgit: Alas, no. I would willingly if I could, but he is hardly ever seen by ordinary fish. He lives at the bottom of the Deep Hole, and seldom comes out. And into the Deep Hole, the lower waters of which are muddy, fishes such as we are afraid to go.

The Doctor: Dear me! That's a terrible disappointment. Are there many of this kind of snail in the sea?

The Fidgit: Oh, no. He is the only one in existence, since his second wife died long, long ago. He is the last of the giant shellfish. He belongs to past ages when the whales were land animals and all that. They say he is over seventy thousand years old.

The Doctor: Good gracious, what wonderful things he could tell me! I do wish I could meet him.

The Fidgit: Were there any more questions you wished to ask me? This water in your tank is getting quite warm and sickly. I'd like to be put back into the sea as soon as you can spare me.

The Doctor: Just one more thing: when Christopher Columbus crossed the Atlantic in 1492, he threw overboard two copies of his diary sealed up in barrels. One of them was never found. It must have sunk. I would like to get it for my library. Do you happen to know where it is?

The Fidgit: Yes, I do. That too is in the Deep Hole. When the barrel sank the currents drifted it northward down what we call the Orinoco Slope, till it finally disappeared into the Deep Hole. If it was any other part of the sea I'd try and get it for you, but not there.

The Doctor: Well, that is all, I think. I hate to put you back into the sea because I know that as soon as I do, I'll think of a hundred other questions I wanted to ask you. But I must keep my promise. Would you care for anything before you go? – it seems a cold day – some cracker crumbs or something?

The Fidgit: No, I won't stop. All I want just at present is fresh seawater.

The Doctor: I cannot thank you enough for all the information you have given me. You have been very helpful and patient.

The Fidgit: Pray, do not mention it. It has been a real pleasure to be of assistance to the great John Dolittle. You are, as of course you know, already quite famous among the better class of fishes. Good-bye and good luck to you, to your ship and to all your plans!

The Doctor carried the listening-tank to a porthole, opened it and emptied the tank into the sea.

'Good-bye!' he murmured as a faint splash reached us from without.

I dropped my pencil on the table and leaned back with a sigh. My fingers were so stiff with writer's cramp that I felt as though I should never be able to open my hand again. But I, at least, had had a night's sleep. As for the poor Doctor, he was so weary that he had hardly put the tank back upon the table and dropped into a chair, when his eyes closed and he began to snore.

In the passage outside Polynesia scratched angrily at the door. I rose and let her in.

'A nice state of affairs!' she stormed. 'What sort of ship is this? There's Bumpo upstairs asleep under the wheel; the Doctor asleep down here; and you making pothooks in a copybook with a pencil! Expect the ship to steer herself to Brazil? We're just drifting around the sea like an empty bottle – and a week behind time as it is. What's happened to you all?'

She was so angry that her voice rose to a scream. But it would have taken more than that to wake the Doctor.

I put the notebook carefully in a drawer and went on deck to take the wheel.

Chapter Three
BAD WEATHER

AS soon as I had *The Curlew* swung round upon her course again I noticed something peculiar: we were not going as fast as we had been. Our favourable wind had almost entirely disappeared.

This, at first, we did not worry about, thinking that at any moment it might spring up again. But the whole day went by, then two days, then a week, ten days − and the wind grew no stronger. *The Curlew* just dawdled along at the speed of a toddling babe.

I now saw that the Doctor was becoming uneasy. He kept getting out his sextant (an instrument which tells you what part of the ocean you are in) and making calculations. He was forever looking at his maps and measuring distances on them. The far edge of the sea, all around us, he examined with his telescope a hundred times a day.

'But, Doctor,' I said when I found him one afternoon mumbling to himself about the misty appearance of the sky, 'it wouldn't matter so much, would it, if we did take a little longer over the trip? We've got plenty to eat on board now, and the purple bird of paradise will know that we have been delayed by something that we couldn't help.'

'Yes, I suppose so,' he said thoughtfully. 'But I hate to keep her waiting. At this season of the year she generally goes to the Peruvian mountains for her health. And, besides, the good weather she prophesied is likely to end any day now and delay us still further. If we could only keep moving at even a fair speed, I wouldn't mind. It's this hanging around, almost dead still, that gets me restless. Ah, here comes a wind. Not very strong – but maybe it'll grow.'

A gentle breeze from the north east came singing through the ropes, and we smiled up hopefully at *The Curlew's* leaning masts.

'We've got only another hundred and fifty miles to make, to sight the coast of Brazil,' said the Doctor. 'If that wind would just stay with us, steady, for a full day, we'd see land.'

But suddenly the wind changed, swung to the east, then back to the north east – then to the north. It came in fitful gusts, as though it hadn't made up its mind which way to blow; and I was kept busy at the wheel, swinging *The Curlew* this way and that to keep the right side of it.

Presently we heard Polynesia, who was in the rigging keeping a lookout for land or passing ships, screech down to us, 'Bad weather coming. That jumpy wind is an ugly sign. And look! – Over there in the east – see that black line, low down? If that isn't a storm I'm a landlubber. The gales round here are fierce, when they do blow – tear your canvas out like paper. You take the wheel, Doctor: it'll need a strong arm if it's a real storm. I'll go wake Bumpo and Chee-Chee. This looks bad to me. We'd best get all the sail down right away till we see how strong she's going to blow.'

Indeed the whole sky was now beginning to take on a very threatening look. The black line to the eastward grew blacker as it came nearer and nearer. A low, rumbly, whispering noise went moaning over the sea. The water which had been so blue and smiling turned to a ruffled ugly grey. And across the darkening sky, shreds of cloud swept like tattered witches flying from the storm.

I must confess I was frightened. You see, I had so far seen the sea only in friendly moods: sometimes quiet and lazy; sometimes laughing, venturesome and reckless; sometimes brooding and poetic, when moonbeams turned her ripples into silver threads and dreaming snowy night-clouds piled up fairy castles in the sky. But as yet I had not known, or even guessed at, the terrible strength of the sea's wild anger.

When that storm finally struck us we leaned right over, flat on our side, as though some invisible giant had slapped the poor *Curlew* on the cheek.

After that things happened so thick and so fast that — what with the wind that stopped your breath, the driving, blinding water, the deafening noise, and the rest — I haven't a very clear idea of how our shipwreck came about.

I remember seeing the sails, which we were now trying to roll up upon the deck, torn out of our hands by the wind and go overboard like a penny balloon — very nearly carrying Chee-Chee with them. And I have a dim recollection of Polynesia screeching somewhere for one of us to go downstairs and close the portholes.

In spite of our masts being bare of sail we were now scudding along to the southward at a great pace. But every once in a while huge grey-black waves would arise from under the ship's side like nightmare monsters, swell and climb, then crash down upon us, pressing us into the sea; and the poor *Curlew* would come to a standstill half under water, like a gasping, drowning pig.

While I was clambering along towards the wheel to see the Doctor, clinging like a leech with hands and legs to the rails lest I be blown overboard, one of these tremendous seas tore loose my hold, filled my throat with water and swept me like a cork the full length of the deck. My head struck a door with an awful bang. And then I fainted.

Chapter Four
WRECKED!

WHEN I awoke I was very hazy in my head. The sky was blue and the sea was calm. At first I thought that I must have fallen asleep in the sun on the deck of *The Curlew*. And thinking that I would be late for my turn at the wheel, I tried to rise to my feet. I found I couldn't. My arms were tied to something behind me with a piece of rope. By twisting my neck around I found this to be a mast, broken off short. Then I realized that I wasn't sitting on a ship at all; I was sitting on only a piece of one. I began to feel uncomfortably scared. Screwing up my eyes, I searched the rim of the sea north, east, south, and west: no land; no ships; nothing was in sight. I was alone in the ocean!

At last, little by little, my bruised head

'I was alone in the ocean!'

began to remember what had happened:
first, the coming of the storm; the sails going
overboard; then the big wave which had
banged me against the door. But what had
become of the Doctor and the others? What
day was this, tomorrow or the day after?
And why was I sitting on only part of a ship?

Working my hand into my pocket, I found
my penknife and cut the rope that tied me.
This reminded me of a shipwreck story that

Joe had once told me, of a captain who had tied his son to a mast in order that he shouldn't be washed overboard by the gale. So of course it must have been the Doctor who had done the same to me.

But where was he?

The awful thought came to me that the Doctor and the rest of them must be drowned, since there was no other wreckage to be seen upon the waters. I got to my feet and stared around the sea again. Nothing — nothing but water and sky!

Presently a long way off I saw the small dark shape of a bird skimming low down over the swell. When it came quite close I saw it was a stormy petrel. I tried to talk to it, to see if it could give me news. But unluckily I hadn't learned much seabird language and I couldn't even attract its attention, much less make it understand what I wanted.

Twice it circled round my raft, lazily, with hardly a flip of the wing. And I could not help wondering, in spite of the distress I was in, where it had spent last night — how it, or any other living thing, had weathered such a smashing storm. It made me realize the great big difference between different creatures, and that size and strength are not everything. To this petrel, a frail little thing of feathers, much smaller and weaker than I, the sea could do anything she liked, it seemed, and his only answer was a lazy, saucy flip of the wing! *He* was the one who should be called the *able seaman*. For, come raging gale, come sunlit calm, this wilderness of water was his home.

After swooping over the sea around me (just looking for food, I supposed) he went off in the direction from which he had come. And I was alone once more.

I found I was somewhat hungry – and a little thirsty, too. I began to think all sorts of miserable thoughts, the way one does when one is lonesome and has missed breakfast. What was going to become of me now, if the Doctor and the rest were drowned? I would starve to death or die of thirst. Then the sun went behind some clouds and I felt cold. How many hundreds or thousands of miles was I from any land? What if another storm should come and smash up even this poor raft on which I stood?

I went on like this for a while, growing gloomier and gloomier, when suddenly I thought of Polynesia. 'You're always safe with the Doctor,' she had said. 'He gets there. Remember that.'

I'm sure I wouldn't have minded so much if he had been here with me. It was this being all alone that made me want to weep. And yet the petrel was alone! What a baby I was, I told myself, to be scared to the verge of tears just by loneliness! I was quite safe where I was – for the present, anyhow. John Dolittle wouldn't get scared by a little thing like this. He got excited only when he made a discovery, found a new bug or something. And if what Polynesia had said was true, he couldn't be drowned and things would come out all right in the end, somehow.

I threw out my chest, buttoned up my collar, and began walking up and down the short raft to keep warm. I would be like John Dolittle. I wouldn't cry. And I wouldn't get excited.

How long I paced back and forth I don't know. But it was a long time – for I had nothing else to do.

At last I got tired and lay down to rest. And in spite of all my troubles, I soon fell fast asleep.

This time when I woke up, stars were staring down at me out of a cloudless sky.

The sea was still calm, and my strange craft was rocking gently under me on an easy swell. All my fine courage left me as I gazed up into the big silent night and felt the pains of hunger and thirst set to work in my stomach harder than ever.

'Are you awake?' said a high silvery voice at my elbow.

I sprang up as though someone had stuck a pin in me. And there, perched at the very end of my raft, her beautiful golden tail glowing dimly in the starlight, sat Miranda, the purple bird of paradise!

Never had I been so glad to see anyone in my life. I almost fell into the water as I leapt to hug her.

'I didn't want to wake you,' said she. 'I guessed you must be tired after all you've been through. . . . Don't squash the life out of me, boy; I'm not a stuffed duck, you know.'

'Oh, Miranda, you dear old thing,' said I, 'I'm so glad to see you. Tell me, where is the Doctor? Is he alive?'

'Of course he's alive — and it's my firm belief he always will be. He's over there, about forty miles to the westward.'

'What's he doing there?'

'He's sitting on the other piece of *The*

Curlew shaving himself — or he was, when I left him.'

'Well, thank heavens he's alive!' said I. '. . . And Bumpo . . . and the animals . . . are they all right?'

'Yes, they're with him. Your ship broke up in the storm. The Doctor tied you down when he found you stunned. And the part you were in got separated and floated away. Golly, it *was* a storm! One has to be a gull or an albatross to stand that sort of weather. I had been watching for the Doctor for three weeks, from a cliff top, but last night I had to take refuge in a cave to keep my tail feathers from blowing out. As soon as I found the Doctor, he sent me off with some porpoises to look for you. A stormy petrel volunteered to help us in our search. There had been quite a gathering of seabirds waiting to greet the Doctor, but the rough weather sort of broke up the arrangements that had been made to welcome him properly. It was the petrel that first gave us the tip where you were.'

'Well, but how can I get to the Doctor, Miranda? I haven't any oars.'

'Get to him! Why, you're going to him now. Look behind you.'

I turned around. The moon was just rising

on the sea's edge. And I now saw that my
raft was moving through the water, but so
gently that I had not noticed it before.

'What's moving us?' I asked.

'The porpoises,' said Miranda.

I went to the back of the raft and looked
down into the water. And just below the surface I could see the dim forms of four big
porpoises, their sleek skins glinting in the
moonlight, pushing at the raft with their
noses.

'They're old friends of the Doctor's,' said
Miranda. 'They'd do anything for John
Dolittle. We should see his party soon now.
We're pretty near the place I left them. . . .
Yes, there they are! See that dark shape? . . .
No, more to the right of where you're look-
ing. Can't you make out the figure of the
black man standing against the sky? Now
Chee-Chee spies us. . . . He's waving. Don't
you see them?',

I didn't – for my eyes were not as sharp as
Miranda's. But presently from somewhere in
the murky dusk I heard Bumpo singing his
African songs with the full force of his enormous voice. And in a little, by peering and
peering in the direction of the sound, I at last
made out a dim mass of tattered, splintered

wreckage — all that remained of the poor *Curlew* — floating low down upon the water.

A hulloa came through the night. And I answered it. We kept it up, calling to one another back and forth across the calm night sea. And a few minutes later the two halves of our brave little ruined ship bumped gently together again.

Now that I was nearer and the moon was higher I could see more plainly. Their piece of the ship was much bigger than mine.

It lay partly upon its side, and most of them were perched upon the top munching ship's biscuit.

But close down to the edge of the water, using the sea's calm surface for a mirror and a piece of broken bottle for a razor, John Dolittle was shaving his face by the light of the moon.

Chapter Five
LAND!

THEY all gave me a great greeting as I clambered off my piece of the ship on to theirs. Bumpo brought me a wonderful drink of fresh water which he drew from a barrel, and Chee-Chee and Polynesia stood around me feeding me ship's biscuit.

But it was the sight of the Doctor's smiling face – just knowing that I was with him once again – that cheered me more than anything else. As I watched him carefully wipe his glass razor and put it away for future use, I could not help comparing him in my mind with the stormy petrel. Indeed the vast strange knowledge which he had gained from his speech and friendship with animals had brought him the power to do things that no other human being would

dare to try. Like the petrel, he could
apparently play with the sea in all her
moods. It was no wonder that many of the
peoples among whom he passed in his
voyages made statues of him showing him
as part fish, part bird, and part man. And
ridiculous though it was, I could quite
understand what Miranda meant when she
said she firmly believed that he could never
die. Just to be with him gave you a wonderful feeling of comfort and safety.

Except for his appearance (his clothes
were crumpled and damp and his battered
high hat was stained with salt water), that
storm which had so terrified me had disturbed him no more than getting stuck on
the mudbank in Puddleby River.

Politely thanking Miranda for getting me
so quickly, he asked her if she would now go
ahead of us and show us the way to Spider
Monkey Island. Next, he gave orders to the
porpoises to leave my old piece of ship and
push the bigger piece wherever the bird of
paradise should lead us.

How much he had lost in the wreck
besides his razor I did not know – everything, most likely, together with all the
money he had saved up to buy the ship with.

And still he was smiling as though he wanted for nothing in the world. The only things he had saved, as far as I could see – beyond the barrel of water and bag of biscuit – were his precious notebooks. These, I saw when he stood up, he had strapped around his waist with yards and yards of twine. He was, as old Matthew Mugg used to say, a great man. He was unbelievable.

And now for three days we continued our journey slowly but steadily southward.

The only inconvenience we suffered from was the cold. This seemed to increase as we went forward. The Doctor said that the island, disturbed from its usual paths by the great gale, had evidently drifted farther south than it had ever been before.

On the third night poor Miranda came back to us nearly frozen. She told the Doctor that in the morning we would find the island quite close to us, though we couldn't see it now, as it was a misty dark night. She said that she must hurry back at once to a warmer climate, and that she would visit the Doctor in Puddleby next August as usual.

'Don't forget, Miranda,' said John Dolittle, 'if you should hear anything of what happened to Long Arrow, to get word to me.'

The bird of paradise assured him she would. And after the Doctor had thanked her again and again for all that she had done for us, she wished us good luck and disappeared into the night.

We were all awake early in the morning, long before it was light, waiting for our first glimpse of the country we had come so far to see. And as the rising sun turned the eastern sky to grey, of course it was old Polynesia who first shouted that she could see palm trees and mountain tops.

With the growing light it became plain to all of us: a long island with high rocky mountains in the middle — and so near to us that you could almost throw your hat upon the shore.

The porpoises gave us one last push and our strange-looking craft bumped gently on a low beach. Then, thanking our lucky stars for a chance to stretch our cramped legs, we all bundled off on to the land — the first land, even though it was floating land, that we had trodden for six weeks. What a thrill I felt as I realized that Spider Monkey Island, the little spot in the atlas which my pencil had touched, lay at last beneath my feet!

HUGH LOFTING

'A long island with high rocky mountains in the middle'

When the light increased still further, we noticed that the palms and grasses of the island seemed withered and almost dead. The Doctor said that it must be on account of the cold that the island was now suffering from in its new climate. These trees and grasses, he told us, were the kind that belonged to warm, tropical weather.

The porpoises asked if we wanted them any further. And the Doctor said that he didn't think so, not for the present – nor the raft either, he added, for it was already beginning to fall to pieces and could not float much longer.

As we were preparing to go inland and explore the island, we suddenly noticed a whole band of Indians watching us with great curiosity from among the trees. The Doctor went forward to talk to them. But he could not make them understand. He tried by signs to show them that he had come on a friendly visit. The Indians didn't seem to like us, however. They had bows and arrows and long hunting spears, with stone points, in their hands; and they made signs back to the Doctor to tell him that if he came a step nearer they would kill us all. They evidently wanted us to leave the island at once. It was a very uncomfortable situation.

At last the Doctor made them understand that he wanted only to see the island all over and that then he would go away – though how he meant to do it, with no boat to sail in, was more than I could imagine.

While they were talking among themselves another Indian arrived – apparently with a message that they were wanted in some other part of the island. Because

presently, shaking their spears threaten-
ingly at us, they went off with the
newcomer.

'What discourteous fellows!' said Bumpo.
'Did you ever see such inhospitability?
Never even asked us if we'd had breakfast,
the benighted bounders!'

'Sh! They're going off to their village,' said
Polynesia. 'I'll bet there's a village on the
other side of those mountains. If you take
my advice, Doctor, you'll get away from this
beach while their backs are turned. Let us
go up into the higher land for the present —
some place where they won't know where we
are. They may grow friendly when they see
we mean no harm. They have honest, open
faces and look like a decent crowd to me.
They're just ignorant — probably never saw
people like us before.'

So, feeling a little bit discouraged by our
first reception, we moved off towards the
mountains in the centre of the island.

Chapter Six
THE JABIZRI

WE found the woods at the feet of the hills thick and tangly and somewhat hard to get through. On Polynesia's advice, we kept away from all paths and trails, feeling it best to avoid meeting any Indians for the present.

But she and Chee-Chee were good guides and splendid jungle hunters, and the two of them set to work at once looking for food for us. In a very short space of time they had found quite a number of different fruits and nuts, which made excellent eating, though none of us knew the names of any of them. We discovered a nice clean stream of good water that came down from the mountains, so we were supplied with something to drink as well.

We followed the stream up towards the heights. And presently we came to parts where the woods were thinner and the ground rocky and steep. Here we could get glimpses of wonderful views all over the island, with the blue sea beyond.

While we were admiring one of these the Doctor suddenly said, 'Sh! A jabizri! Don't you hear it?'

We listened and heard, somewhere in the air about us, an extraordinarily musical hum – like a bee, but not just one note. This hum rose and fell, up and down – almost like someone singing.

'No other insect but the jabizri beetle hums like that,' said the Doctor. 'I wonder where he is? Quite near, by the sound – flying among the trees probably. Oh, if I only had my butterfly net! Why didn't I think to strap that around my waist too. Confound the storm: I may miss the chance of a lifetime now of getting the rarest beetle in the world. Oh, look, there he goes!'

A huge beetle, easily three inches long I should say, suddenly flew by our noses. The Doctor got frightfully excited. He took off his hat to use as a net, swooped at the beetle and caught it. He nearly fell down a precipice on to the rocks below in his wild hurry, but that didn't bother him in the least. He knelt down, chortling, upon the ground with the jabizri safe under his hat. From his pocket he brought out a glass-topped box, and into this he very skilfully made the beetle walk from under the rim of the hat. Then he rose up, happy as a child, to examine his new treasure through the glass lid.

It certainly was the most beautiful insect. It was pale blue underneath, but its back was glossy black with huge red spots on it.

'There isn't an entomologist in the whole world who wouldn't give all he has to be in my shoes today,' said the Doctor. 'Hulloa This jabizri's got something on his leg. . Doesn't look like mud. I wonder what it

He took the beetle carefully out of the and held it by its back in his fingers, w it waved its six legs slowly in the air. We all crowded about him, peering Rolled around the middle section of i foreleg was something that looke thin dried leaf. It was bound on ve with strong spiderweb.

It was marvellous to see how Jo with his fat, heavy fingers undid cord and unrolled the leaf whole, without tearing it or hurting the precious beetle. The jabizri he put back into the box. Then he spread the leaf out flat and examined it.

You can imagine our surprise when we found that the inside of the leaf was covered with signs and pictures, drawn so tiny that you almost needed a magnifying glass to tell what they were. Some of the signs we couldn't make out at all, but nearly all of the pictures were quite plain – figures of men and mountains, mostly. The whole was done in a curious sort of brown ink.

For several moments there was a dead nce while we all stared at the leaf, ated and mystified.

nk this is written in blood,' said the last. 'It turns that colour when it's ody pricked his finger to make es. It's an old dodge when ink – but highly unsanitary. dinary thing to find tied to vish I could talk beetle t where the jabizri got

d. . . . 'Rows of little o you make of it,